Text copyright © 2020 by Tommy Greenwald
Illustrations by Dave Bardin © 2020 Scholastic Inc.

ISBN 978-1-338-30600-2

10 9 8 7 6 5 4 3 2 1   20 21 22 23 24

Printed in the U.S.A. 40

First printing 2020

Book design by Yaffa Jaskoll

Photos © Shutterstock: page i and thoughout: burst (KannaA), page v and thoughout: emojis (Ink Drop).

PROJECT Z

ATTACK OF THE ZOMBIE ZING

TOMMY GREENWALD

SCHOLASTIC INC.

To Phil, Dave, Eric, Daniel, Paul, Christopher, Chiara, John D, Will, Lili, Anthony, Juliana, John V, Christine, James, Thomas, Sofia, and Eddie.

CAST OF CHARACTERS

Arnold: a zombie who now lives among humans; formerly known as Norbus Clacknozzle

Jenny: Arnold's adopted mom; the nicest person you'll ever meet

Bill: Arnold's adopted dad; also the nicest person you'll ever meet

Lester: Arnold's adopted brother, who took some getting used to (he would say the same about Arnold)

Evan, Kiki, and Sarah Anne: Arnold's pals

Ross and Brett: Arnold's not-exactly-pals

Commander Jensen: the commander of the United States Martial Services; friendly

Dr. Grasmere: the head of Project Z; unfriendly

Azalea, Berstus, and Frumpus Clacknozzle: Arnold's former podmates at Project Z

Mrs. Huggle: Arnold's teacher; very sensitive

Nurse Raposo: the school nurse; very supportive

Coach Hank: the gym teacher; very loud

PROLOGUE

I've been through a lot in my short non-life.

I was built by the U.S. government in a secret laboratory, for an undercover operation called Project Z. The program's goal was to create zombies in a secret laboratory, then have them attack American citizens so that those citizens would come together to fight a common enemy—us.

That didn't sound like a lot of fun, so I escaped from the lab. I was eventually rescued by a nice family, who immediately—and for my own protection—made me pretend to be a human boy in elementary school.

Yes, that was as difficult as it sounds.

People thought I was weird—can you blame them? When I made a best friend, it turned out to be a kid whose dad was in charge of the people who were trying to capture me. The dad ended up being really nice, but the authorities finally tracked me down, anyway. They tricked me into going back to the lab by saying I was going to help humans and zombies get along, but all they really wanted to do was turn us into soldiers to fight in wars. Which also didn't sound like a lot of fun, so I tried to escape again and ended up back with my nice family, but I left behind the other zombies who were still stuck in the lab, which made me sad.

So needless to say, it's been complicated, and it's been stressful, and it's been really hard sometimes.

But nothing—and I mean *nothing*—has been as complicated, stressful, and hard as watching my human friend Kiki hold hands with the most obnoxious boy in the entire school, Ross Klepsaw.

Technically, it's true that zombies can't feel pain.

But that one HURT.

THE FRENCH FRY GAME

Lunch was the worst.

The rest of the day wasn't so bad, but *lunch*—that time of day when every kid is basically saying to the world, "These are my people, and they're who I will be spending my precious hard-earned downtime with during a brutal day of learning and reading and writing"—was really hard.

Because I had to sit there, watching Kiki and Ross giggle and gawk and make googly eyes at each other, and pretend that I didn't care.

Actually, I should say *we* had to sit there, because my friend Evan was right next to me.

Don't get me wrong, though. It's not like I liked Kiki— and by like, I mean *like*. No, that wasn't it at all. I'm pretty sure us zombies don't think in terms of that kind of "like." But I was still trying to accept the fact that one of the first and best human friends I'd ever made was now in what could theoretically be called a "romantic" relationship with the one boy who tormented me more than any other human during my early days at Bernard J. Frumpstein Elementary School.

(Sorry. I tend to use big words when I'm upset. I promise never to use the word *theoretically* again. Or *romantic*, for that matter. Instead, I'll use something more age-appropriate. Like *squishy*.)

So yes, I suppose I was a little unhappy about the whole Kiki-Ross situation. But it's not like I lost sleep over it—and not just because I don't sleep. I cared, but not *that much*.

But Evan, on the other hand . . . Evan was a different story.

He was taking it much harder than I was. I think maybe because he did, in fact, feel some of those squishy feelings about Kiki. Not that he would ever admit it, of course.

We were sitting at lunch one day, and it was the same old story. Everyone was enjoying their sandwiches (some kids) or pizza slices (most kids) or fish sticks (a few kids) or tofu salad (Evan) or jelly beans (me) or whatever it was they were eating, and chatting and laughing and occasionally throwing stuff and generally acting like sixth graders.

Except for me and Evan. We were acting like grouchy old men.

Ross, Kiki, and a few other kids were playing a game they called "How many French fries can you balance on your nose?" Ross was the reigning champion. This particular day, he was up to seven, which, when you think about it, is pretty impressive. No one else had managed to pile on more than four.

And then all of a sudden, Kiki got hot. Somehow, she managed to stack up the fries so high, you couldn't even see her eyes. And not one French fry fell! None of us had ever seen anything like it. Even I managed to emerge from my general glumness to marvel at her accomplishment.

"Evan, look," I said, nudging his elbow. "Kiki's on a roll!"

"I don't care," he said, refusing to take his eyes from his food. "Piling French fries on your nose is so dumb. I mean, like, what is this, kindergarten?"

It didn't seem like the right time to remind Evan that we had all played a very similar pile-food-on-your-face game at his birthday last year.

But hold on.

It *did* seem like the right time to remind Evan that his birthday was coming up again pretty soon!

"Hey, Evan, isn't your birthday coming up again pretty soon?"

"I guess," he mumbled. "But I'm not having a party this year."

"Seriously? Why not?"

"Because I don't feel like it." Then, without another word, he got up, put his tray away, and left the cafeteria.

Oh boy. This was worse than I'd thought.

I started to follow him but then walked back to watch

the end of the competition. It turned out that Kiki's stack had reached a grand total of fourteen French fries, a record that was sure to stand until the end of time. Or was it? Because Ross, who disliked losing almost as much as he disliked zombies—at least until he got to know them—wasn't about to give up.

"Last round!" crowed Kiki, reveling in her sure victory.

Ross did some body stretches, as if it were an athletic contest. "Oh, I got this," he said. "There's not a doubt in my

mind you're going down." He grabbed the plate of fries, tipped his head back, and motioned to his friend Brett to start placing the French fries on his nose. The gathering crowd, which now included most of the sixth grade, started chanting along with each fry. Even the teachers and lunch workers craned their necks to see what was going on.

"Four! Five! Six! Seven!"

I glanced over toward the cafeteria exit and happened to see Evan, who hadn't quite left after all. He'd poked his head back in, wanting to see how it ended, just like the rest of us.

"Nine! Ten! Eleven!"

And then—in the blink of an eye, exactly the way most momentous world events happen—the French fries all came tumbling down off Ross's nose and back onto the tray with a soggy plop (they were pretty damp and gross by then).

The contest was over. Kiki had dethroned the reigning champ.

She thrust her arms in the air as the crowd's chant turned to "Kiki! Kiki! Kiki! Kiki!"

Ross bowed before the new champion. "Congratulations," he said. "It couldn't have happened to a nicer person."

And then, from one second to the next, Ross kissed Kiki right on the cheek. And Kiki kissed him back! Right there in front of everyone!

Well, technically, not in front of *everyone*.

Evan had disappeared.

Again.

THE POWER OF CUPCAKES

After a hearty round of congratulations and a victory lap around the cafeteria by Kiki, it was time for everyone to actually finish eating their lunches. And it was also time to mention the topic I'd been waiting patiently to bring up.

I sat down next to Kiki before anyone else could. "Hey, you guys? I have an idea."

Ross slapped me on the back like we were old pals, even though we were new pals—if you can call "hanging around with someone because your best friend has a really annoying crush on them" being a pal.

"Zombie ideas are the best ideas, right, Arnie?"

Yup, he called me Arnie. I'm no more a fan of it than you are. At least it was better than "Ombee the Zombie," which was his other nickname for me.

"Uh, sure, if you say so."

"What's up?" Kiki asked me. She gave me the same

half smile she'd given me on my very first bus ride to school, when I had nowhere to sit until she slid over to make room for me. I will always be grateful to her for that. So grateful, in fact, that I was able to forgive her for what she did next at the lunch table, which was giggle at something Ross whispered to her.

I waited until she stopped giggling, then said, "Evan's birthday is coming up. He just told me he doesn't really want to celebrate this year, but I thought it might be fun if we throw him a surprise party. You know, to kind of cheer him up. I don't know if you've noticed, but he hasn't exactly been in the greatest mood lately."

Kiki's eyes narrowed. "Of course I've noticed." Her head swiveled around. "Where is Evan, anyway?"

"He left." I shrugged. "Guess he wasn't as fascinated with the French fry contest as everyone else."

"What's that supposed to mean?" Kiki knew we didn't approve of her liking Ross. At first she thought it was funny, but as time went on, she found it more and more annoying. "Pardon me for having fun at lunch," she added.

I decided to plow ahead. "So what do you think? About the surprise party, I mean."

"I think it's a great idea!" Ross chimed in. "I really

like that little guy, and he's definitely had a raw deal with that fake leg and all."

"It's not fake," I corrected him. "It's prosthetic, and it works just fine." Evan had cancer as a little boy, and one of his legs had to be amputated. But he moves so easily with his prosthetic leg that it's almost unnoticeable, except when people like Ross bring it up for no reason.

"Okay, sure, whatever," Ross said. "Either way, let's definitely throw him a party. I'm all into that." Ross talked like he thought he was in high school. Which he most definitely was not.

"Great," I said. "Kiki, will you help me plan it?"

"Of course! Do you want to have it at my house?"

"Um, no, I think we should do it at my house. There's a little more room in the yard." I didn't want to say the real reason, which was that I wasn't sure I could get Evan to go over to Kiki's house for *any* reason.

She gave me her brightest let's-all-be-best-friends smile. "Sounds good."

At the end of lunch, I went and found Sarah Anne. She was sitting with Mrs. Frawley, the aide who helps her during the school day.

"We're going to plan a surprise birthday party for Evan," I told her. "Can you help?"

Sarah Anne pointed at letters on her letter board, which was how she communicated with people.

OF COURSE.

"Thanks," I told her. "Maybe we can meet after school tomorrow or the next day?"

YUP. Sarah Anne pointed at the table where Kiki, Ross, and a bunch of other people were still sitting and laughing, then went back to her letter board. WHAT ARE WE GOING TO DO ABOUT ALL THAT?

I shrugged. "We're going to invite them, of course, and hope for the best."

UH-OH.

Mrs. Frawley, who was observing this whole conversation, leaned over. "Can I give you kids one word of advice?" she asked.

We both nodded.

"Cupcakes," said Mrs. Frawley, very seriously.

WHEN YOU SAID ONE WORD, YOU MEANT ONE WORD, Sarah Anne said.

Mrs. Frawley chuckled. "Well, here's a second word for you: *chocolate* cupcakes."

"What about them?" I asked.

"Nothing cuts through tension like baked goods," she said, extremely seriously. "If things get tense and it looks

like the party's going to go south, break out the chocolate cupcakes. Works every time."

I made a mental note to have plenty of chocolate cupcakes on hand for the occasion.

I'd probably have some vanilla and strawberry ones, too, just to be safe.

A SURPRISING dEVELOPMENT

I wish I could say things changed over the next few weeks, but they really didn't. Kiki and Ross didn't get sick of each other, which had been my hope. In fact, the opposite happened; the more they hung around together, the more they seemed to like each other. One day while waiting for class to begin, Ross's best friend, Brett, yanked on my arm.

"So what's the story?" he asked.

"About what?"

"You know." Brett looked around, then leaned in, like he was about to say something secret. "The lovebirds."

I leaned in, too, even though what we were talking about wasn't the slightest bit secret. "Lovebirds? You mean Ross and Kiki? Yeah, I guess they really seem to like each other. Pretty cool, huh?"

"No, not cool at all," Brett said, scowling. "Ross has

changed. He's gotten all...I don't know...what's the word for it...?"

"Nice?" I suggested.

"Ha-ha."

"Well," I said, "I admit it took a little getting used to. I would never have predicted those two would get together, that's for sure."

Brett leaned in again, even closer this time. "Hey, I got an idea. Maybe we should try to break them up. That way, you get your friend back, and I get mine."

"Hey, I got an answer to your idea," I said. "Absolutely not."

Then we both zipped our mouths, because the happy couple was approaching.

"How's it going?" Kiki said.

"What are you guys talking about?" Ross asked.

Brett shifted uncomfortably. "Nothing much, just waiting for class to start. We definitely weren't talking about the two of you, if that's what you're thinking. Not even close."

Seriously, dude?

I shot Brett an annoyed look. "Actually," I said, "we were just talking about Evan's birthday party. Don't forget it's this Saturday night. He thinks he's coming over to my house to watch a movie. Everyone needs to get there by six thirty, because we'll be home by seven."

"Check," said Ross.

"Double check," said Kiki. For some reason, they both thought that was the funniest thing in the world, and they doubled over with laughter. They were still giggling as they walked away.

Brett and I stared at them for a few seconds, and then Brett said, "So like I was saying? Maybe we should figure out a way to make the happy couple not so happy?"

"Let me think about it," I said.

By the night of the party, we had the plan all worked out. My mom, my brother Lester, and I were going to go out to eat with Evan and his family around five thirty. We were going to tell Evan we had to get to the restaurant early to beat the Saturday night crowds. By six forty-five we would head back to our house, where Evan thought we were going to watch *The Jungle Book*—the original one, from 1967, which was one of his favorite movies ever— but instead, a bunch of kids would be waiting to yell SURPRISE! at the top of their lungs.

Unfortunately, things started to go wrong pretty quickly.

The first problem was that Darlene, who was Lester's girlfriend, came to dinner. Under normal circumstances that would have been great, but these weren't normal circumstances. Especially since Lester had forgotten to tell her about the party.

So of course, Darlene rolled in her usual thirty minutes late, despite Lester texting her about sixty-two times.

"Hey, you guys, I'm, like, so sorry," Darlene said, not sounding all that sorry. "My mom said she was going to drive me, but my brother used the car last night, and he couldn't find the keys, and so then my mom and him got in, like, this big fight, and by the time he found the keys she was so mad that she wouldn't drive me, and of course he didn't want to drive me either, so I ended up having to call an Uber and pay for it myself, which is totally unfair if you ask me, right?"

We all just stared at her for a few seconds until my mom, who is tied with my dad for the nicest person ever, said, "Well, we're very sorry to hear that, Darlene. I certainly hope our little dinner for Evan didn't cause you any trouble at home. Go ahead and hurry up and order, dear."

"Yeah," grumbled Lester, not feeling quite as charitable as my mom. "We're gonna be late, thanks to you. This better not ruin everything."

I kicked Lester under the table to make him stop blabbing, but it was too late. "What are you talking about?" Darlene said. "Late for what? And what does 'ruin everything' even mean?"

Lester's face turned a light shade of red as he realized he'd said too much. "Nothing. I mean, you know, it's Evan's birthday, so we want to make sure that, you know, we can get to the store and get a cake before it closes or something."

Darlene stared at Lester. "I'm sorry for being late, like I said, but you are totally not making any sense at all right now." She turned to Evan. "Dude, happy birthday, by the way. And I promise you, we are going to get you the sweetest cake you've ever seen."

Evan, who had been watching this whole exchange with the liveliest expression I'd seen on his face in weeks, nodded vigorously. "Oh, I'm not worried about it, Darlene. Tonight's not even my birthday—tomorrow night is—so if I don't get a cake tonight, I'm sure I'll get a great one tomorrow."

"Of course we're getting you a cake tonight," my

mom said. "It's the night-before cake."

"Too bad you can't have any, Mr. Jelly Bean Man," Lester said to me with a hint of irritation still in his voice. Even though we basically got along really well, whenever he was mad about something—or mad at someone—he tended to take it out on me by reminding me that I was, in fact, a zombie. And zombies, as everyone knows by now, can only eat jelly beans.

"Be nice to your brother," my dad said. He didn't tolerate any kind of fighting, and especially any kind of fighting in public.

"Semi-brother," Lester mumbled.

"What did you just say?" My dad's voice had taken on a new level of intensity.

"Let's everyone just calm down," said my mom. "This is a celebration, remember?"

"Should I go?" Darlene asked.

"Maybe," Lester said.

"You stay right there," my mom ordered.

"Yes, ma'am," Darlene said.

"This is going great so far," my dad said. I was pretty sure he was kidding.

I caught Evan's parents glancing at each other. They hadn't said anything during this entire exchange, but now it seemed like they'd had enough. "Okay," said Mr. Brantley. "Perhaps it's best if we head out and leave the Kinders in peace to work things out, shall we?"

I was thinking to myself that actually that wasn't a bad idea, when Mr. Brantley gestured to his wife and son. "Honey? Evan? Shall we?"

Huh?

I realized with a slight jolt of horror that Mr. Brantley didn't know about the surprise party.

Evan stood up glumly. "I really wanted to see that movie. And have cake."

"We'll have cake tomorrow," his dad reminded him.

Luckily, before the night turned into a complete disaster, Mrs. Brantley saved the day. "Horace, why don't you and I go, but let Evan stay," she said. "I've been meaning to try out that new ice cream place downtown, anyway."

Mr. Brantley thought for a second. "Do they have rocky road? You know I love rocky road."

"I'm sure they have rocky road, honey."

"Fine." Mr. and Mrs. Brantley got up. "Evan, we'll pick you up later," said Mr. Brantley. "Enjoy your party."

Wait, did he just say that out loud? Now I was really confused. Did he know about the party or not? Either way, he was blowing it big-time.

Evan's eyes crinkled. "What party?"

"Ha-ha-ha-ha-ha-ha!" tittered Mrs. Brantley, way too excitedly. She yanked on her husband's arm. "That's tomorrow night, dear; you know that!"

"Wait a second," Evan said. "I said I didn't want a party, remember?"

I sank lower in my chair. Things had gotten way out of hand, and we hadn't even gotten our drinks yet.

"Not *party*, exactly," said Mrs. Brantley. "Just a family

gathering, that's all. Tomorrow night. Just the family."

As I stared at Evan's mom with grateful appreciation, I thought about what she was like when I first met her. It was hard to believe she'd been the one to turn me in to the authorities way back when.

Boy, times had sure changed.

"Okay," Evan said, but he still looked suspicious. "I'm just not really in the mood for a party these days. I thought I was pretty clear about that. And don't even think about a surprise party, because that would be worst of all."

Luckily, the waiter came right then, and we could change the subject once and for all.

"Who's ready to order?" he said.

Evan raised his hand. "I am. I'd like to order everyone at this table to not throw me a party."

It was starting to look like it was going to be one of those nights.

Luckily, we got through the rest of the meal okay. Darlene and Lester made up, the food was delicious (everyone was oohing and aahing over the fried chicken, which did look delicious, even to a zombie), and by the time we paid the check and headed out to the car, Evan was excitedly singing the lyrics to "The Bare Necessities."

That's a song from *The Jungle Book*, which was the movie that Evan thought we were going to be watching when we got back to my house, but which we weren't, because we were throwing him a surprise party, which he'd told us earlier would make him very upset.

But hey, a plan's a plan, right? So there we were, in the car on the way home, when I texted Kiki: **We'll be there in 10 min.**

We're ready! she texted back. **This is going to be so AWESOME!**

I wasn't sure what to say to that one, so I just let it lie.

As we drove up the driveway, I noticed the house was dark. As in, *completely* dark. Unnaturally dark. Everyone leaves at least one or two lights on even when they're not home, right? But this was pure blackness.

"Jeez, your house is really dark," Evan said, right on cue.

"We must have forgotten to leave a light on!" shouted everyone in the car, basically at the same exact time. Evan looked a little startled at our group enthusiasm, but luckily didn't seem to put two and two together.

My mom opened the front door and went in first. She

turned a light on in the kitchen. We followed her. The house was deadly silent. We all stood there for a few seconds, each waiting for someone else to say something. It was the most awkward moment in the world. If someone wrote a book on how to throw a surprise party, I'm pretty sure the first rule would be, "Don't walk into your own house and freeze in place as if you're in a play and you've forgotten your lines."

But still, Evan was clueless. "What time do you want to start the movie?" he asked. "My mom is picking me up at nine thirty."

Lester, bless his heart, was the first one to step up to the plate. "Hey, Evan," he said, "can you go into the living room and grab the big bowl that's on the coffee table? I'm gonna rustle up some popcorn."

"You bet!" Popcorn always got Evan excited, since it was the one semi-unhealthy treat his mom let him eat.

Sure enough, Evan raced into the living room, turned on the light, and was greeted by a room full of sixth graders leaping up from behind couches, chairs, and tables, and all screaming, "SURPRIIIIISEEEEE!"

Evan froze in place like he'd seen a ghost. Or, more accurately, about twenty-five ghosts.

Kiki, Ross, Brett, and all the other kids in our homeroom class charged at Evan, yelling "Happy birthday!" and "You're the man!" and "You should have seen your face!" and stuff like that. Sarah Anne waited until all the chaos had died down a bit, then went over and gave Evan a hug.

I stood in the doorway, scared stiff, waiting to see how Evan would react to the exact thing he'd said earlier he didn't want.

After five seconds that felt like five years, I had my answer: A giant smile crossed his face.

"YESSSSS!" he crowed. "A SURPRISE PARTY! LET'S DO THIS!"

And so I was reminded once again you can never take anything an eleven-year-old human boy says too seriously.

Even if he's about to turn twelve.

It Was Fun until It Wasn't

I have to hand it to my parents: They broke out all the greatest hits for Evan's party.

We had a popcorn machine, because I remembered he'd loved it at his birthday party last year. We had a karaoke machine, so everyone could sing their favorite songs (I confess, I have not been able to adjust to this whole thing they call "pop music." It's really just a series of random noises, with someone singing words that are often impossible to understand.) There was a little dancing, a little flirting, a lot of hot dogs, a water balloon fight, two kinds of cupcakes (chocolate and vanilla), and a make-your-own-caramel-apple station.

Evan was in heaven.

As the party was winding down, I thought we were home free, because everything had gone perfectly. As some kids started to get picked up by their parents, Lester made the perfectly innocent suggestion of playing

a pickup basketball game in the driveway while everyone else waited for their rides.

"Under the lights, it will be sweet!" he said. "Evan
and Arnold, you guys be captains." Even though only a
few kids were still there, it was a little thrilling to be
asked to be a captain of anything sports-related. It didn't
exactly happen every day.

Evan picked Ross, and I picked Lester, and Evan
picked Kiki, and I picked a tall girl named Angie, and
Evan picked a kid named Philip, and then we both realized that the last one standing there was Brett.

He didn't look happy.

"Are you guys serious?" he moaned. "I'm, like, usually
one of the first kids picked."

"Well, now you know how it feels to be one of the last
kids picked," said Evan. He was obviously feeling a little
bolder than usual, it being his party and all.

"You're on my team, Brett," I said, and he harrumphed
his way over to my side of the court.

"I'll ref," said my dad cheerfully.

It was the last cheerful thing anyone said all night.

It turned out Brett wasn't kidding when he'd said at
school that he wasn't happy about Ross and Kiki. They
were both on Evan's team, so Brett decided that it was

the perfect excuse to make their lives miserable, at least until someone's mom or dad came to pick them up.

First, he tripped Ross.

"Foul!" announced my dad. "Brett, that was uncalled for. It's a friendly birthday party pickup game, not game seven of the NBA finals."

"Sorry, Mr. Kinder," Brett said, but he didn't seem all that sorry, especially since two plays later, he gave Kiki a healthy push from behind, and she went sprawling into the bushes.

"HEY!" screamed Ross. "You just pushed a girl! *My* girl! That was so not cool!" And he gave Brett a healthy shove of his own. But Brett didn't go sprawling into the bushes, he went SPLAT! onto the concrete driveway, and came up clutching his arm and wailing.

"I think I broke my elbow!" he moaned. "I mean, I think *you* broke my elbow!"

"The game is over!" bellowed my dad. "Everyone, back inside!"

Angie and Philip followed my dad over to Brett to see if he was okay, while Kiki dashed over to Ross and put her hand on his shoulder, as if to say, *It's not your fault, honey.*

Evan, who was standing there with his mouth open, trying to figure out how the end of his party went so wrong, saw Kiki and Ross huddled together and decided that was the last straw.

"That's it! I'm sick of this! I'm sick of you two just being all lovey-dovey and ignoring everyone else! Kiki, I thought we were best friends, and you know that Ross and Brett have been making fun of me for, like, forever, but you just don't care, and now he just broke Brett's arm, and you're still standing there next to Ross like he's so awesome, and I don't want to be friends with any of you guys anymore, and this was the WORST BIRTHDAY PARTY EVER IN THE HISTORY OF THE WORLD!"

And right then, as if on cue, Evan's mom drove up the driveway, and without another word Evan ran to the car and got in. Mrs. Brantley got out of the car and was on her way up the front walk, probably to say thank you to my parents for the party, when Evan stuck his head out the window.

"MOM! LET'S GO! HURRY UP! I WANT TO GO!"

My mom ran over to Mrs. Brantley. "I'm so sorry," she said. "There was a minor incident at the end of the party. I'm sure it will all be fine, but Evan got a bit upset. You should probably get him home."

Mrs. Brantley nodded and gave my mom a quick hug, then went back to her car and got in. Evan stared straight ahead as they backed out of the driveway.

The rest of us stared as they drove away. Brett, who'd forgotten all about his supposedly broken elbow, kicked the basketball into the yard. No one said anything until Sarah Anne, who'd been watching this whole thing from the porch, walked over to us with her letter board.

HE FORGOT HIS PRESENTS.

A VISITOR

I didn't see Evan for a few days after that, except in school. We all decided it was best to leave him alone. At lunch, he sat by himself, at the same table and in the same seat he had been sitting in when I saw him on my very first day of school. He was even eating the same unidentifiable healthy gloopy green stuff.

Ross and Brett made up, of course. In fact, they made up about thirty seconds after Evan left in a huff. Kiki helped by telling Brett that even if she and Ross liked each other, Brett and Ross would always be best friends. Brett seemed to accept that. It turns out even obnoxious kids get their feelings hurt every once in a while.

As for my parents, well, let's just say they've decided that maybe we'll hold off on surprise parties for the foreseeable future. Which is just fine with me.

And Lester? He thought the whole thing was hilarious. I believe his exact quote was, "Holy smokes, that whole thing was hilarious!" But later that night, when he realized that I was actually really sad about losing my best friend—at least temporarily—he knocked on my door and sat down on my bed.

"Sorry about today," he said. "Fighting with friends can be a real drag. But it never lasts."

"I guess," I told him. "But it wasn't just today. Something's been up with Evan for a while. At first I thought it was because of Kiki and Ross, but I'm not sure anymore. Maybe it's something else."

Lester lay back on the bed with a big plop. "Well, give the little dude his space, and eventually he'll be ready to tell you what's up. Aaaite?"

Lester said *aaaite* a lot. Humans use it as a faster way to say *all right*.

Five minutes after Lester left my room, I got a text from Evan: **Sorry about today. I didn't mean to ruin the party. I have a lot on my mind, I guess. Thanks for everything.**

Wow, I thought to myself. *Maybe Lester is right!*

It's okay! I texted back. **Do you want to talk about it?**

It took Evan about five minutes to respond.

No.

Two days later, I was walking home from school when I got a text from my mom: **Are you on your way home?**

I scratched my head in confusion. That was a weird question. I almost always came home right after school.

Yes, I responded.

My mom texted again: **Great!**

· My mind jumped to the possibility that maybe Evan was at the house. Although that didn't make sense, since Evan was anti-me right now.

Why? What's up?

Just hurry home.

Is something wrong?

NO!

Excitement surged through my bloodless veins. I started to run before remembering that running and me didn't get along. So I walked as fast as my rubbery legs could take me, and made it home in about ten minutes. I would have been out of breath, but I don't breathe.

I turned the corner to our street and saw an army vehicle in our driveway.

That would have made me stop breathing, but again, a quick reminder—I don't breathe.

But just because I don't breathe, and can't run, and have no warm blood in my body, it doesn't mean I can't feel emotion. And the emotion I was feeling right at that moment was fear.

Intense fear.

It was the exact kind of military vehicle—a jeep, with darkened windows and a deep green paint job—that they had in the Territory. Those were the vehicles that were driving all over campus looking for me when I was trying to escape. I'd learned to not like those vehicles.

So why was one at our house?

I had a flashback to the last time I'd had this feeling about someone visiting our house. It was when Dr. Grasmere, the director of Project Z, had come to convince my family and me that I should go back to the Territory to help the zombies enter regular society. I'd agreed. Big mistake.

I walked slowly up the front steps and opened the door, pretty sure I wasn't going to like what I saw.

But I was wrong.

Because sitting there, having coffee with my parents, was Sergeant Kelly—the nicest human person in the whole Territory. She protected me when everyone else was against me. And she helped me when I thought I was going to be punished for trying to escape.

"Sergeant Kelly!" I exclaimed. Then, without thinking, I ran up to her and gave her a big hug.

"Oh!" she said, in a voice of awkward surprise. That was when I realized that maybe you weren't supposed to run up and hug sergeants in the United States Army.

I immediately pulled back and said, "Whoops! Sorry about that. I was just . . . happy to see you, I guess."

Sergeant Kelly laughed. "Oh, it's all good," she said. "I'm not exactly a stickler for regulations, and what harm can one hug do, right?"

"Right," I said.

My parents were sitting on the couch, but unlike when Dr. Grasmere visited, they didn't seem tense at all. In fact, they were both smiling broadly.

"Sergeant Kelly has come to see us with an interesting piece of news," said my mom.

"That's right," my dad chimed in. "The big cheese wants to see us."

"The big cheese?" I scratched my head. I had no idea what that meant.

Sergeant Kelly had an envelope in her hand, and she held it out to me. "Here, take a look at this."

I took the envelope—the first thing I noticed was some type on the back, in big red letters:

EXPEDITED DELIVERY FROM THE UNITED STATES ARMED FORCES

And then, just below that, in black letters:

COMMANDER JONATHAN JENSEN, USMS

"What does USMS stand for?" I asked Sergeant Kelly.

"United States Martial Services."

"Go ahead and read it," my mom said.

I grabbed the letter from the envelope and read it in about 3.5 seconds. (I'm a really fast reader, especially when I'm excited.)

Dear Mrs. Kinder, Mr. Kinder, and Arnold,

I hope you have all been well.

I wanted to give you an update about where things are with Project Z.

We have been making great strides in planning for our next phase.

I think you will be excited to hear what we are thinking.

It would be my great pleasure to host you all at my quarters for a meeting, which can be arranged at your convenience. Refreshments will be served.

It will be very good to see you all again, and I send you my best regards.

Sincerely,

Jonathan Jensen

Regional Commander, United States Martial Services

I held the letter out to my parents.

"We've already read it," said my dad.

"So?" said my mom. "Pretty cool, right?"

They must have thought a look of excitement would cross my face, because they seemed confused when it didn't.

"Arnold?" said my dad. "Everything okay, buddy?"

I wasn't sure I wanted to say what I was thinking out loud, but everyone was waiting for me to speak, so I did.

"I don't want to go."

You could hear a slight gasp from my mom. Sergeant Kelly, however, didn't look surprised at all.

My dad gently put his hand on my shoulder. "Can I ask why not?"

"Because the last time someone came to visit us to ask us to go back there, it was a trick. This might be a trick, too. I don't ever want to have anything to do with any of those people ever again." I looked at Sergeant Kelly. "No offense, Sergeant."

"None taken," she said.

"Well, let's talk about this for a second," said my mom. "I completely understand what you're saying, Arnold, and I don't blame you one bit. The last experience was traumatic for all of us. But this is different. This is the head of the entire operation inviting us to his residence, which isn't even in the Territory. He ended up helping us, remember? I honestly think this is going to be good news, and we should consider it."

"You said that last time," I reminded her.

My mom blinked twice. "That's right, I did."

"Okay, I'll consider it," I said. "Do we have to decide right now?"

"Of course not." My mom turned to Sergeant Kelly. "Thank you so much for stopping by. We will think about this very generous request and get back to you shortly."

"Sounds good," said the sergeant. "It was good to see you all again. Arnold, you seem terrific, and I'm so glad everything is working out for you."

"Thank you," I said. And then I added, "Can I ask you what you think, Sergeant Kelly? Do you think we should go to meet Commander Jensen?"

Sergeant Kelly thought for a second. "I'm not in a position to offer advice in these kinds of situations," she said. "It's above my pay grade. But I will tell you this: Commander Jensen is among the most honorable people I have ever met in the armed forces."

And with that, she saluted and left.

My parents and I stood there for a few seconds. I decided they were waiting for me to say something, but I wasn't sure I had anything to add. Finally, an idea popped into my head. It was a way to deal with the two most important things on my mind at the same time.

"I'm going over to Evan's house to ask what he thinks."

EVAN'S NEWS

I wasn't going to call Evan and ask if I could come over, because I was pretty sure what he was going to say.

No.

So instead, I found myself standing on his front stoop, ringing the bell.

His mom answered the door.

"Arnold! What a nice surprise!" She glanced around her, and then pulled me inside. She motioned me to follow her into the kitchen.

"What are you doing here?" she whispered.

"Uh, I came to see Evan. I'm sorry, I should have called."

"No, no, it's fine." She rubbed her hands together nervously. "It's just that—well, today is kind of a big day."

"It is?" For a second, my heart lifted, as I thought she meant something good was about to happen. But then I saw the expression on her face, and I realized immediately that wasn't the case. "Oh . . . um . . . is everything okay?"

"Yes, yes . . . well . . . it's better I let Evan tell you." Mrs. Brantley walked to the edge of the stairs and called up. "Evan? Honey? Arnold is here to see you!"

We waited a few seconds, but there was silence.

"Arnold would very much like to say hi!"

Still nothing.

Mrs. Brantley looked at me. "Go on up," she whispered.

"Are you sure?"

"Of course I'm sure." She smiled a bit sadly. "He might not realize it, but he'll be very glad to see you."

I walked up the stairs, not sure if I was doing the right thing. Why was I insisting on seeing Evan when he was going out of his way to not see me?

I guess because we're friends, that's why.

The door to his room wasn't quite shut all the way. There was only a dim light shining through—I thought maybe he was trying to sleep.

I knocked softly.

"Come in."

I went into the room and saw Evan on his bed, reading a book. He didn't look up.

"Hey," I said.

"Hey," he said.

I sat down on the chair near his desk and waited for around a minute. It was a long minute. Then I said, "So I wanted to tell you that Sergeant Kelly from the Territory—remember, she was the nice one you met? Anyway, Sergeant Kelly came to our house today, and she brought a letter from the commander, this guy Commander Jensen, and the letter said that he wants us to go meet with him to discuss some exciting new things that are happening, and he wants us to go to his house and eat dinner and stuff, but I'm still pretty nervous about it, though, because the last time someone from the Territory came to see me, it was a trick, and I almost got trapped back there forever, and so I don't think I want to go, but my parents think I should go, and I wanted to know what you thought since you're my best friend."

Evan closed his book, looked up at me, and said, "I have cancer again."

You know how sometimes it feels like the air leaves a room, and the walls are closing in, and suddenly it's really hot and you can't breathe?

Well, at that moment, I felt all of that, except the can't-breathe part.

"Uh, what?" I said, because they were the only sounds that could come out of my mouth.

"I have cancer again." Evan swung his legs over the side of the bed, giving a little extra push to his prosthetic leg. He looked at me for the first time. "I have these regular checkups, and a few weeks ago I had this small bump on my hip, and they did tests on it, and last week the doctor told me that it was cancer. When they amputated my leg, they said they were hopeful that the cancer was gone for good, but that sometimes it spreads a little bit and you don't find out until later, and I guess that's what happened."

"Why didn't you tell us?" I managed to ask.

"I don't know, I guess I didn't feel like it." Evan had a new energy in his voice, almost like he was relieved that he'd finally told somebody. "It's like, I feel different enough already with my leg, you know? And a lot has been going on, and it was my birthday, and I just—I guess I just didn't want to be, like, the guy who everyone feels sorry for again."

"I get that." I thought back to Evan sitting alone at lunch, and me thinking he was just grouchy about Kiki and Ross liking each other, and throwing him that birthday party that went south really fast, and I suddenly had a heavy feeling in my chest. "And I'm really sorry."

"Don't be." Evan gave me a reassuring pat on my knee. "You were just trying to be a good friend, and I really appreciate that."

The heaviness lifted a bit. "Cool." We sat there for a second, and then I asked, "So what happens now?"

"Well, now I have to deal with hospitals and tests and treatments and stuff. Today I found out what kind of treatment I'm going to get, and that I might lose my hair because of it. I didn't mind losing my hair when I was three, but you know in middle school it's pretty much the worst thing ever."

I had no idea what he was talking about in terms of losing his hair, but it didn't seem like the right time to ask. "Well, I'm sure you know this already, but I'm happy to do whatever you need, and so are all your friends."

"I know," Evan said. "I guess I'll tell the rest of the guys tonight. Now that I've talked about it, I feel better."

"I'm glad."

He stood up. "You want to go outside and shoot baskets?"

"Sure!"

And just like that, we were friends again. But it wasn't the same—it couldn't be the same. Evan had a new battle to fight, and I wanted to be there to help him every step of the way.

We shot baskets for a while. Well, to be more accurate, we shot *at* the basket, because I would say probably about 7 percent of our shots went in. Then Evan said, "What was it you were saying before? You know, before I rudely interrupted you by saying I had cancer again?"

"Ha-ha." I didn't exactly feel like talking about myself at that moment. It felt a little selfish given the circumstances, but it seemed like Evan really wanted to know.

"Uh, well, what I was saying was, my family and I got a visit from Sergeant Kelly, and Commander Jensen wants to see us and tell us some exciting news, but I feel nervous about going because of what happened last time."

Evan shot the ball, and it missed as usual. I caught the rebound, shot, and also missed as usual. Evan caught the rebound and threw the ball into his garage. "That's enough of that."

"I couldn't agree more."

We sat in two chairs on his front lawn and both gazed up at the sky, which was a bright blue except for the occasional puffy white cloud. It was one of those perfect days, except for what was actually going on in the world.

"I get why you're nervous," Evan said. "But you always trusted Sergeant Kelly, right?"

"Right."

"And Commander Jensen is the one who let you go back to your family, right?"

"Right."

Evan took a sip of the healthy green gloop his mom always made him drink. "I think you should go."

I was shocked. "You do?"

"Yes."

It took me a few seconds to absorb his opinion. And a few seconds after that, I had an idea.

"Okay, I'll go. But you have to come with me."

It was Evan's turn to be shocked. "What are you talking about?"

"Think about it." I turned to face him, squinting because of the bright sun. "If you come with me, that will be like having an outside witness. They would never do anything to me with you there."

"Huh," Evan said, pondering.

"And I think your dad should come, too. Then they'll never try any funny stuff." Evan's dad used to have Commander Jensen's job, but he'd become one of my fiercest protectors, so he wouldn't let them get away with anything.

Evan got up out of his chair and mulled over what I'd said for a few seconds. Then he nodded. "Sounds like a plan."

"Yes!" I said. I got up out of my chair, and we high-fived, but I saw Evan wince a little bit. "Are you okay?"

"Oh yeah, absolutely," he said. "I guess I'm just a little tired, that's all. I get tired pretty easily these days."

I suddenly felt embarrassed that I'd taken up his time yapping about myself when he could be in his room, resting. "I'm really sorry I came over and bothered you with this."

"Don't be!" Evan stared up at the sky for a second, then looked back down at me. "Remember what I said. I don't want anyone to feel sorry for me. I'm the same old annoying kid I've always been."

"Excellent," I said. "So I'll look forward to you being annoying in school tomorrow?"

Evan smiled for the first time that day. "You can count on it."

STOP BEING SO NICE

Evan wasn't annoying at school the next day, though, because he's not an annoying person. And by lunch, pretty much everyone knew about the return of his cancer, but we all did our best not to show any pity for him or feel sorry for him.

The only problem is that we kind of did the opposite—we showered him with affection and attention until it was a little ridiculous. Especially at lunch.

It started with Brett, who saw Evan come into the cafeteria and immediately ran up to him. "Evan, dude! Sit with us!" Not that Evan had much of a choice, since Brett grabbed one arm, Ross grabbed the other, and they guided Evan to a seat between them.

"Do you need anything?" Ross asked. "Maybe some fish sticks, or an ice cream sandwich?"

"No, thanks, I'm good," Evan said. "My mom doesn't let me eat that stuff, anyway."

"Got it!" Brett looked at Evan like a puppy who was eager to please. "Your mom's so smart! It's really important to eat healthy; I need to get on that."

"Take it back a notch there, cowboy," said Kiki, but two seconds later, she said, "Evan, let me know if you need a fork or a spoon or anything." Then, realizing how that sounded, she added, "You know, only because I'm going up there, anyway. Of course, you can get your own fork or spoon—or knife, even. I am in no way suggesting that you can't."

"Who's the cowboy now, cowboy?" Brett said, smirking, and he had a good point.

Evan, meanwhile, just kept drinking his green gloop with a slightly embarrassed smile on his face.

Later on, in gym, Coach Hank took things up a notch past Brett's notch. "EVAN!" he bellowed. "You're my captain! In fact, you're my captain for the rest of the year! For every sport!"

"But I don't want to be the captain for the rest of the year," Evan protested. "For *any* sport."

"Really?" Coach Hank looked confused. "But it's a perfect job for you! You know, because you can't actually participate anymore."

"Yes, I can," Evan told him. "I can definitely

participate. In fact, I am going to be the same horrible athlete I've always been."

"OKAY, SUPER!" Coach Hank blasted his whistle. "Everybody, LINE UP! Evan is going to lead calisthenics today!"

"I am?"

"You ARE!"

Evan sighed deeply. "Okay, everyone do twenty jumping jacks."

"We'd love to!" said half the class, while the other half said, "You got it, Evan!"

We all did our jumping jacks, although mine were horrible and Evan's weren't much better.

"Okay, uh, now everyone do ten push-ups."

"Anything for you, Evan!" said half the class, while the other half said, "You're doing a great job so far!"

And that was when Evan had had enough. He stopped mid-push-up—I think it was his second or third—and got to his feet.

"Um, I just need to say something."

The rest of us stopped our push-ups.

"Yes, I have cancer again. And yes, I'm really thankful that no one is looking at me with pity, or feeling sorry for me, or acting sad."

Everyone nodded, feeling good about themselves.

"But, um . . . I have to say that everyone being extra nice and extra friendly is kind of almost as bad. Meaning, it's still treating me . . . I don't know, differently. What I really want is for everyone to just treat me like you always do."

And with that, Evan got back on the floor and resumed his push-ups. No one was quite sure what to do or say, so we all just stood there, doing nothing. Finally, Ross raised his hand.

"Can I say something?" he asked.

"GO AHEAD!" barked Coach Hank.

Ross pointed at Evan, who was struggling mightily on the gym floor.

"Those are the absolute worst, most pathetic push-ups I have ever seen in my LIFE."

All the kids cracked up, especially Evan.

And just like that, everything was back to almost normal.

A SURPRISE ANNOUNCEMENT

When I told my parents I was willing to go meet with Commander Jensen, they were surprised, and pleased.

When I told my parents I wanted Evan and his dad to come with me, they were surprised, and confused.

"Why?" said my mom. "This was a direct request to you, and us, from the U.S. government and the U.S. Armed Forces. It's not the kind of thing where you can just add a plus-one."

"Or plus-two," added my dad.

"I understand," I told them. "However, I won't go unless they come with us."

My parents looked at each other and sighed. "I'll talk to Horace," said my mom. "I'm sure he can make a few calls and figure it out."

"And I want Lester to come, too," I said.

My mom nodded. "Of course."

"Do you want me to see if your teachers and nurses

and Coach Hank can come, too?" said my dad. "Maybe we can make it a party."

"Ha-ha," I said. "And also, yes, I'd love that."

All kidding aside, everything worked out fine, because a week later, we were on our way to Commander Jensen's headquarters—my parents, Lester, and me, plus Evan and his dad. Lester, who hadn't seen Evan since he'd told us about his medical situation, handled it in true Lester fashion.

"Yo, Evan, you look great!" he said. "You getting to skip school and stuff?"

"Sometimes, when I have to get treatment."

"Sweet!" Lester exclaimed. Then, suddenly realizing how that sounded, he added, "I mean, you're one coura-geous dude, of course. But nothing wrong with missing a pop quiz here and there, am I right?"

Evan couldn't help but smile. "I guess."

"Can we change the subject?" my mom asked.

"Sure!" Lester ruffled Evan's hair. "So is it true that you might be kissing these gorgeous locks good-bye?"

My parents rolled their eyes at each other, but Evan didn't seem to mind. "Yep," he said. "One of the side effects of the treatment will probably be that I lose my hair."

"Dude, you don't realize it, but that is really good news," Lester said. He noticed the pained expressions on all of our faces. "No, seriously!"

"Okay," Evan said, not sure where Lester was going.

Lester pulled out his phone. "Let's look up 'famous bald men.' See, check this out. Michael Jordan, only the best basketball player EVER."

Evan's eyes went wide. He was a huge basketball fan, even though he wasn't exactly headed for the NBA anytime soon.

Lester scrolled through his phone. "Bruce Willis and Vin Diesel, two awesome actors. And yo, Dwayne Johnson! The Rock! And LL Cool J! Come on, you guys, being bald has never been cooler."

"Or hotter," added my mom.

My dad gave her a look. "Excuse me?"

"I'm just saying," she said, and everyone laughed.

Evan's dad put his hand on Lester's shoulder. "Comparing my son to Michael Jordan may be the nicest thing anyone has ever done for him. Thank you for that."

"Anytime," Lester said. "I mean, I'm just saying,

things that seem bad at first sometimes turn out to be not so bad."

"That's very wise, Lester," said my mom. "And very true."

We'd been driving for about forty-five minutes when we finally turned onto a road that had a giant security gate blocking it. There was a big sign over the gate:

AUTHORIZED PERSONNEL ONLY

We pulled up to the guard booth, where a soldier came up to our car and rapped on the window.

"May I help you?"

My mom, who was driving, stuck her head out the window. "We're here to see Commander Jensen."

"Name and identification, please."

My mom handed the soldier her driver's license.

"I'm going to need everyone's identification, ma'am."

"Even the minors?"

"Everyone, ma'am."

So my dad and Mr. Brantley got out their driver's licenses, too, Lester got out his high school ID, and Evan and I got out our library cards. The soldier took them all, looked them all over, and went into the little booth and made a phone call that took about thirty seconds. Then he came back out and returned our stuff.

"You're good to go," he said. He pointed to a big truck-type thing up ahead of us. "You'll be escorted to the commander's quarters. Just follow the forward vehicle. Have a good day."

"Holy smokes," said my dad, looking at the truck. "That is one sweet Humvee right there."

"It's the standard armored vehicle escort that all VIP guests receive when visiting the commanding officer," said Mr. Brantley, and he would know, since he used to *be* the commanding officer.

"We're pretty important, ya know," my mom added.

Almost every structure inside the compound was a brick building, but we pulled up to a lovely big white house, with a fence and a lawn and lots of beautiful trees. Outside, gardeners were planting flowers, and someone was painting one of the black shutters that framed the windows.

As we got out of the car, we all uttered some form of "Whoa."

Two soldiers guarded the front door as we went inside. We were brought into a giant room that had an enormous wooden table in the middle, and bookshelves that must have held about a thousand books.

"Hey, Arnold, it would take you at least a week to read all the books," cracked Lester.

"Please make yourselves comfortable," said one of the soldiers who had shown us in. "The commander will be with you shortly."

"Can anyone actually get comfortable in this place?" my mom wondered out loud. "Give me our itty-bitty house any day of the week."

We all laughed, or tried to. The truth was, I was a little tense. I think we all were, but I *know* I was. Government buildings made me nervous, even ones as pretty as this.

After another minute or so of trying to stay calm, I heard sharp footsteps outside the door. The soldier who was in the room with us immediately sprang to attention. He was suddenly by far the tensest of all of us!

Then the door opened, and the commander walked in.

He was a little older than I'd remembered: His hair was white, which was the complete opposite of his dark jacket uniform, which had medals all over the front. Just the look of him scared me for a second, but as soon as he saw me, his face broke into a big smile.

"Arnold!" he said. "What a true delight it is to see you again!" And he came over and shook my hand. He had a strong grip. I don't have a strong grip. For a second I thought he might pull my arm clear off.

Commander Jensen made his way around the room, greeting everyone. Finally he motioned for us all to sit at the enormous wooden table. He sat at the head, of course.

"I'm so pleased that you could all come to visit," he said. "I know you all lead very busy lives, and I appreciate you taking the time to make the drive." He was acting like we were doing him a favor, even though he was the commander of the whole southwest district! It was pretty funny, now that I think about it.

Commander Jensen took a sip from the cup in front of him which was probably tea, since that's what we all had in front of us, except me: I had a bag of jelly beans on a plate. And water.

We waited for him to finish his drink. My mom smiled at me. I tried to smile back.

"So I have some exciting news," the commander said. "We've been working very hard; and more importantly, so have the afterlife humans in our care. They've been making tremendous progress. And last week, at our monthly update summit, it was agreed that we would consider the idea of assimilating another subject into mainstream society."

Commander Jensen paused. We all looked at one another with varying degrees of surprise on our faces—except for Lester, who just looked confused, probably because he didn't know what *assimilate* meant.

Mr. Brantley was the first of us to respond. "Well, I'm sure I speak for all of us here when I say how excited we are to hear that. I know the program has had a lot of ups and downs, which I myself was a part of, so if it turns out that it will indeed prove beneficial, that would be such welcome news for all of us."

"Excellent, Horace," said the commander. "I'm so glad you feel that way."

"That's wonderful news," my mom said. "I always knew there was merit in this program. And even if it took a while, it now seems all the hard work was worth it."

"Indeed, Jenny," agreed the commander. "Indeed it was."

There were a few more questions and answers, and some more conversation about the program, but there was only one thing I was dying to know (well, not *dying*, but you know what I mean). I was pretty sure everyone was thinking the same thing and had the same question, but it didn't seem like anyone else was going to ask, so finally I raised my hand. "Excuse me, Commander Jensen?"

"Yes, Arnold?"

I tried to clear my throat. "Well . . . uh, sir, I, uh . . . I heard you say that you had made the decision to assimilate another subject. And, well, I was wondering if you knew who that subject was going to be."

Commander Jensen smiled, showing his really white teeth. "I must say, I thought you'd never ask!" He stood up and walked over to a door that I hadn't even noticed before, because it was built into the bookcases. It almost looked like a trapdoor you'd find in one of the television mystery shows that my dad liked to watch.

The commander made a fist and rapped on the door, three times quickly. It began to slide open.

"Ladies and gentlemen," he said, "may I present to you the next afterlife human who is ready to enter the real world."

And out walked Azalea Clacknozzle.

My eyes went wide with shock as an electric buzz pulsed through my body. *Azalea!*

She was the only other juvenile in the Territory besides me. I'd become good friends with her when I was there the second time. My brain had been programmed to only remember very specific things, but I remembered her. I remembered everything about her.

"Hi, Azalea," I said, my voice barely above a whisper. "Do you remember me?"

Azalea was clearly very nervous, and spent a few seconds looking at everyone, blinking a lot, trying to figure out where she was and what exactly was happening to

her. But when she saw me, I could see her body relax. And she smiled, just a little bit.

"Yes, you're Arnold," she said softly. "Hello, Arnold."

It was interesting to hear her call me Arnold. She'd only ever called me "Norbus" in the Territory. Norbus, as in Norbus Clacknozzle, my original Project Z name. But we weren't in the Territory anymore. We were out in the real world. Me, and now her. The two of us. I wouldn't be the only one anymore.

"Welcome," I told her. "Welcome to ..." I wasn't quite sure what to call it ... what it was to be outside, in the real world, with real humans. It took me a few seconds to come up with the right word.

"Welcome to freedom."

AzALEA'S NEW HOME

So, yeah, I have cancer again. Now that we've gotten that out of the way, is it okay if we don't talk about it very much? Or at all?

If it has something to do with the story, then fine, I'm happy to discuss it. But if not, then I'd just as soon put it away.

Great.

So where were we?

Oh yeah. "Welcome to freedom," Arnold said, and then he and Azalea stared at each other like they couldn't believe their eyes. I was pretty sure they were going to run into each other's arms, like you might see in some sappy movie, but instead the two of them just stood there, like they were afraid to move.

"Thanks," Azalea said finally.

The commander guy with the white hair and cool military uniform clapped his hands together, almost like he was trying to break some kind of spell or something. "Terrific!" he barked. "I knew this would be a surprise to beat all surprises! But now we have work to do."

"What kind of work?" asked Arnold's dad.

"Well," said the commander, "for one thing, we need to figure out where to place Azalea. Ideally, it will be in the same community as Arnold is, which is why I've brought you all here today. I'd like your advice and input, if you have any to offer."

I noticed Arnold's parents look at each other, and for a split second I thought they were going to offer to take Azalea, too! I saw Arnold look at them, too, and I could tell he was thinking the same thing. But before anyone got any ideas, Mrs. Kinder said, "Of course we will keep that in mind, Commander. As you know, we have our hands full with Lester and Arnold, but I'm sure there will be a family who will be gracious enough to take on this rewarding assignment."

"We'll have to do background checks, of course." The commander looked at my dad. "But if any of you have someone you would recommend, that would go a long way toward getting this approved and underway."

My dad nodded. "I'll certainly give it some thought."

The adults continued to talk, trying to figure out the best way to place Azalea in the right home. After a few minutes, Lester got bored and took out his phone. He was all set to start doing the stuff people usually do on their phones when a soldier came over with a stern look on his face. "No devices in Commander HQ," the soldier said. Lester, who looked like he'd seen a ghost, put that phone away super fast.

I glanced over at Arnold. "Pretty cool, huh? Your friend Azalea getting to come out of the Territory?"

"Awesome," Arnold said. "I just hope we can figure out where. If no one wants her, they might put her somewhere else, in some other town, or maybe even forget the whole thing altogether."

"Yeah, I know." We both smiled at Azalea, who kind of smiled back. I tried to imagine what it must have felt like, sitting there, listening to a bunch of people decide your life for you—or your afterlife, in her case—but realized I couldn't. I definitely couldn't imagine how hard it must have been to be her, not knowing what was going to happen to you.

"How about if we take her?" I heard someone say.

All heads turned in my direction. It took me a few seconds to realize that the "someone" was me.

My dad smiled and started to say something like, "Ev, I don't know if that's—"

But I cut him off. "I know there are a bunch of reasons to say no. I know that it's crazy, and I know how stressful it would probably be, and all the things that could go wrong, and how this is probably the exact opposite of how I should be taking care of myself, being sick and all. I get all that. But I still—well, who else would do it? Who's a better choice than us?"

I was looking at my dad, but I heard Arnold whisper to Lester, "That would be so awesome."

"I—I don't know," my dad said. "I need to talk with Mom, of course. She would have a strong opinion about this, I know that much." He laughed a little at the thought of telling my mom that they might need to make room for one more person at the dinner table. Permanently.

Commander Jensen cleared his throat and looked at my dad. "Horace, the last thing I want to do is make your life difficult, especially with what your boy here is going through. We will certainly explore all options available to us, and I'm sure we'll find a suitable home."

"I appreciate that, Commander," said my dad. "In any event, we don't want to make any hasty decisions.

These things need to be thought out and discussed thoroughly."

I looked at Azalea, who was sitting by herself at the end of the table, swiveling her head back and forth, just listening. She looked so shy and awkward, on the outside looking in. She reminded me of me. I knew how hard it was going to be for her. Which was why I wanted to help her.

"Dad," I said, "I know what Mom is going to say. I know she's going to want to protect me and say this is the last thing I need. But this is the *exact* thing I need. It will be a good distraction for me, and give me something to do other than worry about getting better. And I will get my rest." I glanced over at Azalea again. "Helping her will help me. I promise."

My dad let out a deep sigh, which I knew was a good sign. "I'll think about it," he said, which I knew really meant, *I'll try to talk Mom into it.*

Three days later, we brought Azalea home.

AN uN-BLAST FROM THE PAST

For the first couple of days after Azalea moved in, all we did was show her around town, help her get used to her surroundings, and teach her all about the ways of the human.

Arnold was over a lot to help, of course. He taught Azalea how to put her contact lenses in (to cover up the red streaks across her pupils that would probably freak people out), told her how often she should raise her hand in class (not that often), showed her what sunscreen was, stuff like that. He taught me and my parents a lot, too, like what kind of paper towel worked best to clean up zombie sweat, and how to make a jelly bean smoothie.

After about ten days, my parents announced that Azalea was ready to go to school the following Monday—and to celebrate, we were going out to dinner.

"You're going to make your debut!" my mom said to Azalea. "It's a new day! We don't have to hide you, and

you don't have to hide yourself. Just be proud of who you are."

Azalea didn't talk much, but when she did speak, her vocabulary made Arnold sound like a dummy. "I'm highly anticipating my inaugural venture into the public eye," she said. "I just hope I acquit myself honorably."

"Right," I said. "But can you repeat that in English?"

Azalea looked at her feet, which she did a lot. "I'm looking forward to it."

We went to a restaurant called Eldrick's, which had the best fried chicken on the planet, in my opinion.

Unfortunately, the first word in "fried chicken" is *fried*, and one of my mom's rules was no fried food. Fortunately, this was a special occasion, so the rules didn't apply.

We walked into the restaurant, ordered our food, and sat down. Nobody batted an eye at us. Everything was going perfectly. Azalea, sitting there in her sweatshirt and jeans, looked like a skinny, pale version of everyone else, and no one seemed to notice that she wasn't human.

We had just started eating when a man wearing a red jacket walked into the restaurant. He looked slightly familiar, but I wasn't sure why. Azalea didn't notice him at first, but then she glanced up and saw the man, and her whole body stiffened up like a lunch tray.

My dad noticed, too. "Azalea? Is everything okay?"

Azalea didn't say anything; she just pointed. My dad turned, saw the man, and immediately got up from the table.

"Horace, what's going on?" asked my mom, but my dad didn't answer. He just started walking toward the man. I think my dad was trying to intercept him, but he was too late. The man spotted us and headed right to our table.

"Well, well, well!" said the man in the red jacket. He seemed perfectly friendly to me, but the look on Azalea's and my dad's faces told me otherwise. "How nice it is to see you all again!" He turned his gaze to Azalea. "And I heard about all this exciting new development. Hello, young lady. Might I say, you look perfectly lovely out here among the living."

My dad quickly returned to his seat. "Everyone, this is Dr. Grasmere, the former head of research and development at the Project Z laboratory. Azalea, you know him, of course."

Suddenly, it came back to me. I did know this guy. He was the one who tricked Arnold into going back to the Territory, and then tried to keep him there forever.

"I thought you were fired," I said before I could help myself.

"Evan, watch your manners," whispered my mom.

But Dr. Grasmere only laughed. "There are no firings in the federal government, my young friend, only reassignments," he said. "And yes indeed, I was reassigned. I'm no longer part of the direct Project Z team, but I'm delighted to say I'm still involved, as an official observer. So I shall be keeping a close eye on things, and reporting back to my colleagues in Washington, who I must say are very skeptical about this whole business of integration and assimilation." He glanced over at Azalea. "Not that I blame them."

So *that's* why this guy was here. He was spying on us! Because he wanted the whole thing to fail!

"Thank you for stopping by," said my dad, not sounding particularly thankful at all. "Now, if you don't mind, I'd like to get back to our family meal."

"Family?" Dr. Grasmere said. "Oh, yes, of course. *Family.*"

"We ARE a family, whether you like it or not," I said. "You already tried to destroy Arnold's life, and we're not going to let you destroy Azalea's."

The doctor smiled, showing his yellow teeth. "I admire your gumption, young man, and your loyalty. But I have to take exception to one thing you said. Your friend Arnold—or whatever his name is—and your new family member Azalea here do not have lives. They have *systems*. They are our creations, our inventions. Some creations work out, and some don't. And occasionally, when they don't work out, you have to destroy them." Dr. Grasmere bowed, as if he had finished a performance. "And now I will leave you to enjoy the rest of your meal."

After Dr. Grasmere walked away, we all sat there in silence for a few seconds. Then Azalea said, "If I am putting you all in an untenable position, I would gladly return to the Territory."

I didn't know what *untenable* meant, but I was pretty sure I knew what she was saying.

"You're not going anywhere," my mom said. "Except to school tomorrow."

I ordered a hot fudge sundae for dessert, but it didn't taste as good as I thought it would.

AzALEA, mEET ALICE

Being the new kid in school is never easy. But being the new zombie kid in school? That must have been a whole different ballgame.

We'd taken Azalea to the school a few times, to show her what it was like and to help her get used to it. But I don't think she was fully prepared for walking in on the first day and being surrounded by hundreds of screaming kids. I saw her eyes bulge out of her head when she saw one kid give another kid a noogie on his head, and then the second kid return the favor by pinning the first kid's arms behind his head so a third kid could tickle the first kid's armpits until he laughed so much he turned purple.

Azalea turned to me. "Do you know those boys?"

"Yep," I answered. "They're on the math team, which won the State Math Olympiad last year."

She looked confused. "So what you're saying is that they're . . . smart?"

"Correct."

Azalea shook her head and followed me down the hallway, toward Mrs. Huggle's room. Halfway there, we ran into Arnold, Kiki, and Ross, who were standing in the hallway, laughing at some joke Kiki had just told.

"Hey, you guys," I said.

Arnold, who of course knew Azalea, smiled widely. "You made it!" he cried. "Sweet! This is gonna be awesome!"

"You converse in a very different manner than you did in the Territory," Azalea told him.

"You know it," Arnold said. "When in Rome, as they say."

"As who says?" Ross asked.

"Never mind," I said. I needed to make introductions. "Kiki, Ross, I'd like you to meet Azalea. She just moved here from . . . well, from where Arnold moved here from."

"Pleased to make your acquaintance," Azalea said.

"Yours, too!" Kiki said. "I remember seeing you when we rescued Arnold! I know you're going to love it here, just like Arnold does."

Azalea looked unconvinced. "I hope so."

Ross stuck his hand out. "So are you going to zap me stiff, too?"

Azalea cocked her head sideways, like a confused dog. "I'm not sure I know what you mean."

"Oh yeah," Ross said, wincing at the memory. "Your buddy here once froze me in place just by pinching my neck."

"That's because you had me pinned up against a locker with no way out," Arnold reminded him.

Ross snickered. "Yeah, well, I still say total paralysis was a bit of an overreaction, don'tcha think?"

A light bulb went off in Azalea's head. "Ah, yes. You must mean the Zombie Zing. I'm very familiar with that technique, although I'm pleased to say I've never found it essential to employ."

As soon as Azalea started to speak, Ross rolled his eyes. When she finished, he rolled them again, in case anybody had missed it the first time. "Oh, here we go. Another super vocabulary genius straight from the zombie factory. Can you learn to talk normal like Arnold did?"

Kiki flashed her dark eyes at him. "Knock it off, Ross."

But Ross was just getting started. "Since you talk all fancy-schmancy, maybe you can help me with my homework, like your buddy Arnie here."

"Ross!" Kiki had raised her voice a bit, and that was

all it took. Ross dropped the attitude and stuck out his hand. "Nice to meet you."

Azalea shook it a bit nervously. "Nice to meet you, too."

I elbowed Kiki in the ribs. "How do you get Ross to listen to you like that?"

"Simple," she said. "He knows who's boss."

Mrs. Huggle, our teacher, was sitting at her desk when we walked in.

"Aha," she said. "My new student. Welcome. Everyone, this is Azalea Clacknozzle, who has enrolled in our school. She, like Arnold, is an afterlife human."

There was a bit of murmuring at that, and I heard the word *zombie* whispered a few times.

"You know the drill," continued Mrs. Huggle. "Be nice. Be courteous. Be welcoming. Behave."

Azalea took a seat in the front of the room as people smiled courteously at her. She smiled back. Ross and Brett kept quiet. So far, so good.

Mrs. Huggle held up a sheet of paper. "Before we begin our lessons, I want to mention that today is one of the most special days of the whole year." She waved the sheet of paper in the air. "It's sign-up-for-the-school-play day! Yay!"

The rest of the class did not exactly share her enthusiasm, but Mrs. Huggle didn't care. "This year, we'll be doing a production of *Alice in Wonderland*. Who would consider signing up to be a part of this wonderful production?"

Five girls and zero boys raised their hands. One of the girls was Kiki—she always got the best parts, of course. But this was the one thing that Kiki couldn't get everyone else to follow her on. Getting kids to do the school play wasn't easy. Getting male kids to do the school play was practically impossible.

"People!" cried Mrs. Huggle. "You can't be serious! This is one of the finest stories in all of literature, and there are some great acting parts here!"

But no more hands went up. Mrs. Huggle sighed. "Well, I get it. You're all busy with language lessons and tutoring and sports and other stuff. But the sign-up sheet will be right here when you change your mind."

She was in the middle of taping the sheet to the wall when another hand went up.

Azalea's.

"What is acting?" she asked.

Mrs. Huggle looked up in surprise. "How lovely to hear your voice, Miss Clacknozzle. Acting, my dear, is when you pretend to be someone else." She shifted her eyes from Azalea to Arnold, then winked. "Your good friend here, Mr. Ombee, did an excellent job of acting when he first joined our community. But now he is able to be himself, as you are, and it's so much better this way."

Azalea thought for a second, and then raised her

hand again. "I would like to act as Alice in your production of *Alice in Wonderland*. I would like to feel what it's like to not be myself."

The class was silent as we absorbed what Azalea was saying. It must have been really hard to be her. Which must have been why she wanted to be someone else— even if it was only pretend.

Mrs. Huggle nodded with a kind smile on her face. "I understand completely, Azalea, and I think it's wonderful that you would like to join our play. However, I cannot award the part of Alice to you—or to anybody, in fact—without an official audition process. It's the only fair way."

Kiki raised her hand.

"I would like to suggest we don't do auditions for Alice, and just award the part to Azalea."

A murmur went through the classroom as people tried to take in this information. Was Kiki—the girl who always got the best parts—willingly giving up the limelight to this strange new semi-person?

She was.

Arnold raised his hand. "I agree with Kiki, although I know that's easy for me to say since I'm not a girl and wouldn't be trying out for that part, anyway."

"I agree, too," Ross said. "And I am also not a girl."

The class tittered at that.

Mrs. Huggle hushed the class. "This is certainly a nice gesture of generosity, but I cannot make the decision by myself. We would need to put it up to a vote. Raise your hand if you would like to award Azalea the opportunity to play Alice in our classroom production of *Alice in Wonderland.*"

Kiki's hand went up right away. Five other hands went up, including Arnold's, Ross's, Brett's, and Sarah Anne's. I raised my hand, too. Then slowly, every other hand in the class went up.

"Well," said Mrs. Huggle. "It's unanimous. Democracy at work, right?" She walked over to Azalea and put her hand out. Azalea shook it. "Congratulations, Azalea," said Mrs. Huggle. "Or should I say Alice?"

"Azalea is fine," Azalea said, but for the first time, the rest of the class got to see her smile.

mALL TImE

At lunch, Arnold had an idea.

"When I was just learning the ways of humans," he said, "my family took me to the mall, and it was a very valuable experience. I discovered that there were very many different kinds of jeans, and stores that liked to play music very loud, and there were a lot of people who were enjoying not doing much of anything, which I realized was an important activity for teenagers, and it's where I met Darlene and helped Lester talk to her."

Kiki, Azalea, Ross, Sarah Anne, and I were all sitting there, listening to this speech. After Arnold finally stopped talking, Ross raised his hand. "That's all terrific, Arnie. What's your point?"

Arnold rolled his eyes—a trick he'd learned from Kiki, who was a master—as he finished chewing a jelly bean. "My point is that I think we need to take Azalea to the mall."

Azalea immediately shook her head. "I'm not ready."

"Yes, you are!" Arnold insisted. "You've been here almost two weeks. I went to the mall after, like, five days."

"What does 'like five days' mean?" Azalea asked.

Kiki giggled. "People say 'like' a lot, for, like, no reason."

"You just did it," I pointed out.

"Ha, I guess I did!"

Azalea had more questions. She always had more questions. "Why do people use words for no reason?"

We were all stumped on that one, except Sarah Anne. She took out her board. BECAUSE WE'RE WEIRD, she said.

"Oh," said Azalea. "That makes sense."

"We're not weird," I said, feeling a sudden need to defend the human race for some reason. "But we do sometimes say things that are kind of weird. Like 'yeah, no.' People say that a lot."

Kiki nodded. "And 'a hundred percent,' which is just a longer way of saying 'yes.'"

Ross suddenly decided this was a game, and he wanted to play. "'Dude,'" he said. "I say 'dude,' like, all the time."

"You do?" Kiki asked, pretending to be surprised.

He nodded. "A hundred percent."

Kiki punched Arnold's shoulder. "When Arnold first got here," she said, "he talked as if he were Mr. Oxford Dictionary himself. But now he uses 'like,' like, all the time."

Azalea turned to her fellow zombie. "So in order to assimilate into society, I should also start using these words?"

"Absolutely not," Arnold said. "Not, like, if you can help it." Then, catching himself, he added, "Dang it!"

"So anyway," I said, "about the mall."

"Oh yeah, right." Arnold popped an orange jelly bean into his mouth. "I can get Lester to take us after school. Darlene still works at the store, and I think taking Azalea is a good idea, both to show her what it's like and to maybe get her some new clothes."

Azalea looked herself up and down. "Is there something wrong with my wardrobe? Am I wearing something ill-fitting?"

"I think you look fine," I said, although no one had ever once called me any kind of a fashion expert, that's for sure.

Kiki was beginning to see what Arnold was too polite to say directly. "I think what Arnold is trying to say is, like, you're doing really well, but you still seem a little nervous, a little, like, formal—maybe going to the mall and relaxing and trying on some different kinds of clothes will help you feel a little more at home."

"Yes, that's exactly what I'm saying," Arnold said, nodding at Kiki gratefully.

Azalea looked at me. "Evan, do you think it would be okay with your parents?"

"I think it'd be more than okay," I said.

😵 😎 😜

Two days later, Arnold, Kiki, Ross, and I took Azalea to the mall, which was basically a bunch of stores with only a few people inside them, and lots of wide, long hallways with many people in them.

"Let's head there," Arnold said. He was pointing at a store called Boyz Cloze. The music was blaring, which didn't make any sense to me. Even if you liked the music, how was the salesperson supposed to hear you when you asked for a shirt? I didn't get it.

Also—in case you couldn't tell, I'm kind of a sheltered person. My parents haven't let me do that much stuff. I could probably use the same kind of loosening-up practice that Azalea needed.

"Let's do this!" I said. I was trying to sound

enthusiastic, but I was pretty sure I wasn't pulling it off.

We went into the store, and the first person we saw was Darlene. She was folding shirts, and, man, was she good at it. She folded about ten of them in twenty seconds, and every one looked perfect. Darlene got plenty of practice working here and at its sister store across the mall, Kidz Cloze.

This week, her hair color was a deep, dark blue.

She looked up and gave us a huge smile. "Well, lookie here!" she said. "Just the people I need to brighten my dull day working in retail purgatory."

Azalea and Arnold both laughed at that, probably because they were the only ones who knew what *purgatory* meant.

Darlene went right over to Azalea. "It is so good to see you again," she said. "I heard you'd moved in with the Brantleys, which is so exciting. Another zombie in our midst. Awright!"

"Thank you," Azalea said, slightly nervously. Even though she'd met Darlene on the day we brought Arnold back from the Territory the second time, she seemed a little unsure what to make of this blue-haired high school girl.

"We're here to get Azalea some clothes," I said, trying to move things along. My mom was picking us up in an hour.

Darlene looked confused. "Huh? You do know this store is called Boyz Cloze, right? The first word in the title is *Boyz*."

"Yeah, we know," Kiki said. "But for one thing, I thought it would be fun to visit you here, because you're so cool, and for another thing, I wear boys' shirts all the time." She pointed at herself, and the long button-down blue shirt she was wearing. "Like right now."

"So you are." Darlene nodded her approval at Kiki's choice. "Well done." She pulled on Azalea's arm. "Okay, come with me."

While they walked over to look at some shirts, the rest of us browsed around the store, trying to hear ourselves think over the music. Then I saw Kiki and Ross walk out of the store, and I felt those annoying old pangs of jealousy again. I hurried over to where Arnold was staring at a pair of jeans.

"Why do these pants have so many rips?" he asked. "Shouldn't they get that fixed?"

I shook my head. "That's the style—the more rips, the better. Now come with me."

Arnold didn't seem satisfied with my answer—not that I could blame him—but he came with me, anyway. We watched as Kiki and Ross wandered across the hall, to where the mall movie theater was playing a movie called *Floodthirsty 3-D*.

"Whoa, what's that movie about?" Arnold asked.

"I'm not exactly sure, although I did hear some kids at school talking about it. I think it's about a giant space creature who tries to take over Earth by making the oceans overflow into the cities."

"Yikes."

"Yeah."

Arnold was still staring up at the marquee. "And what does *3-D* mean?"

"It means you put on these weird glasses, and it feels like the action in the movie is right in front of you and coming toward you."

"Cool," Arnold said, which is a word he never would have used when I first met him.

Ross and Kiki, meanwhile, had spotted us and were coming back over. "We should totally go see this movie," Ross said. "It looks awesome."

"It looks the opposite of awesome," Kiki said. "But it does look ridiculous in a fun kind of way."

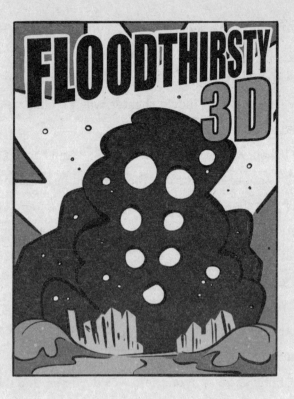

I looked at the clock on my phone. "My mom is coming soon."

"Can't you text her?" Kiki asked. "Maybe she can come in, like, two hours? We'll still get home in plenty of time for dinner and homework and stuff."

"Please?" Ross begged.

Meanwhile, Azalea and Darlene were coming out of the store, with Darlene grinning from ear to ear and Azalea wearing a shirt about two sizes too big for

her, ripped jeans, and a beanie like the type skate-
boarders wear.

She looked pretty awesome, I had to admit.

"I hooked this lady UP!" hollered Darlene. "I mean,
how fly does she look?"

"Extremely fly," Arnold said.

"I'm assuming that fly is good?" Azalea asked, speaking for all of us.

"Very," confirmed Darlene. "What are you guys doing
out here? Thinking about going to see *Floodthirsty*?"

I said "Not really" and Kiki said "Definitely" at the
same exact time.

Unfortunately, Darlene came down on the side of the
wanna-sees. "Oh man, I saw it last week," she said. "It's
awesome." She said it in such a way that made me realize
I would be the definite bad guy of this story if I said we
couldn't see it.

"Ugh," I said. I got out my phone to text my mom.

**Hey. Everyone wants to stay and see a movie.
It's only 2 hours. Can we??**

I never had to wait long for my mom to text back.
Twenty seconds later:

You have homework.

I can do it after.

Which movie?

Floodthirsty

When does it start?

10 minutes

When is it over?

5:15

What is it rated?

PG

Are you sure Azalea can handle it?

Very sure.

This time there was a longer pause. She was obviously mulling it over. We all stood there, waiting.

Okay, fine. I'll be there at 5:20. Be outside by the double doors. Don't keep me waiting.

OK! Thanks!

I gave everyone the thumbs-up, which led to a general buzz of excitement.

I gave Darlene my credit card for the clothes. "Nah, I got it," she said. "Friends and family discount. You can get me later."

"Really?"

"Really."

Things were looking up. Then Ross Klepsaw, the kid who had pretty much made my life miserable for the previous six years, held his hand up for a high five. I smacked it.

"Your mom rocks, dude," Ross said. "And so do you."

Things had sure changed around here.

SCARY MOVIE

It took about five minutes for me to realize that going to see the movie was a bad idea.

There was a scene where the alien guy, who looked like a horned toad with an extra head sticking out his back, first comes to Earth. He lands in a swamp, shakes his body dry, then screams and sprints directly toward the camera.

Meaning directly toward *us*.

In the 3-D glasses, it looked so real! I was so scared I jumped out of my seat, but then I pretended I was just stretching my legs, because my friends didn't seem scared in the slightest. In fact, Kiki and Ross were laughing their heads off.

"This is hilarious!" hollered Ross. It was clear he had a disturbed sense of humor.

"It's the funniest thing ever!" agreed Kiki. It was clear I had to reconsider my opinion of Kiki.

Arnold didn't seem scared or amused. He just seemed confused by the whole thing.

"Is this your first time in a movie theater?" I whispered to him.

He nodded. "I've watched movies at home with my family, but this is the first time in a giant dark room with a bunch of other people," he said. "It's weird."

"You'll get used to it," I said. Then I glanced over at Azalea, who was sitting there with her mouth wide open. "Azalea? Are you okay?"

She didn't say anything, but she shook her head. Her eyes never moved from the screen.

"Hold on," I said. "Are you saying you're *not* okay?"

She shook her head again.

"Well then, what are you saying?" I asked, which was kind of a silly question, since she wasn't saying anything. I decided to just leave her alone.

A few minutes later, Kiki passed me her popcorn. I took a handful and shoved it in my mouth, but was surprised to taste something soft, squishy, and not popcorn-y at all.

"Ugh!" I said, apparently too loudly, because someone in the row in front of us turned around. He was an adult and didn't look too happy.

"Hey, will you kids keep it down back there?" whispered the adult. "This is a movie theater, not a playroom."

"Sorry," I said. "Won't happen again." I tapped Kiki on the shoulder a little aggressively. "There's something wrong with your popcorn!"

"There's nothing wrong with it," she whispered back. "It's got Raisinets in it. Popcorn and Raisinets are the perfect combination!"

My immediate reaction was to be grossed out, but as I continued to chew, I realized she had a point. The salt-and-chocolate mixture was actually quite delicious.

"Hey, you're right," I whispered. "This is really—"

But I never finished my sentence, because at that exact moment, the space alien creature guy began attacking his first city, flooding it with his secret toxic orange liquid. The people in the city started turning orange, then growing second heads out of their backs, just like the creature. Then suddenly they all looked like aliens and started acting like aliens, too, stomping around and looking for other innocent people to dump the toxic sludge onto. It was really scary. I forgot about the popcorn.

Even Kiki and Ross weren't laughing anymore.

We were all on the edge of our seats, except Azalea, who was still sitting exactly as she'd been sitting the whole time, with her mouth wide open.

Then the new army of aliens started marching forward, with their arms stretched out toward us. They each had two heads and were covered in orange muck. They started running. In our 3-D glasses, it looked incredibly real. I mean, I knew it wasn't, of course, but that didn't stop me from cowering in my seat anyway, looking for someplace to hide. I think I heard a person scream, and I think that person might have been me.

Then, when the creatures were practically on top of us, one rose up and leapt at the screen. It was like he was leaping right into our laps!

"AAAARRRRGGGGHHHH!!!" The whole theater started screaming hysterically. Except for one person. Well, technically, not quite a person.

Azalea.

Instead of screaming, she rose up out of her seat, leaned forward, and reached out to pinch the creature in the neck. Unfortunately, the creature was still on the screen, so she ended up pinching the neck of the person sitting in front of her.

And that person—the one who told me to stop acting

like we were in a playroom—suddenly froze in place.

Yup.

Azalea had Zombie Zing'd him.

That's what Zombie Zings do, remember? They freeze people in place. But usually, the people who are zing'd are attacking the zombie who zings them. In this case, the person was just watching the movie.

But I guess Azalea thought she was being attacked. And I can't really blame her.

At first, no one noticed the frozen guy, except me. Not even the people he was with! Everyone was too focused on the crazy scary stuff happening on the screen. But I knew I needed to do something, because Azalea was still standing there, as if she were in a trance, and I was worried that she might try to Zombie Zing someone else. The last thing we needed was a theater full of frozen people.

So I ran up the aisle and found an usher. "I'm sorry, but there's a problem!" I said. "You have to stop the movie!"

The usher, who looked like I had just woken him up from a nap, barely looked at me. "You'll have to go ask the manager," he said. "Also, this is the good part."

"Where can I find the manager?"

"Uh . . ." he said, and I didn't stick around for the

answer. I ran out into the lobby and found somebody with a name tag. "Are you the manager?"

She looked at me suspiciously. "I might be."

"You need to stop the movie! There's been an accident! Someone is hurt!"

That got her attention. "Hurt? Meaning, like, they're choking on popcorn or something? Like, we could be sued?"

"No, nothing like that!" I started to tell her what happened, then realized that was a bad idea. "Just stop the movie, and we can straighten it all out."

She scratched her head. "I'm not sure what you mean."

"JUST STOP THE MOVIE!" Well, the sight of a kid screaming at her must have finally done the trick, because she got out her walkie-talkie and mumbled, "We have a situation, code blue in the theater. Please halt the showing." Some garbled message came back five seconds later, but she must have understood it, because she told me, "Okay, the movie's been stopped. Now take me to this situation."

I hurried back into the theater, with the manager right behind me. Inside, everyone was standing up, stretching their legs, and complaining about what was going on. We ignored them and ran up the aisle to where I'd been sitting. The people in our area were just starting to discover that there was a frozen man in their midst.

The woman who must have been the guy's date was pointing and babbling hysterically. "What happened to Josh? Oh no! Josh? Josh? JOSH? What happened to Josh? He's not moving! Somebody help us! The movie must have really freaked him out! Josh, are you okay?"

Meanwhile, the frozen guy, whose name was apparently Josh, was darting his eyes back and forth, since those were the only parts of him that could move.

I ran up to my friends, who also seemed frozen in place, but only because they were not sure what to do.

"Guys! Guys!" I hissed. "What are you doing? Arnold, Azalea, do something! Un-zing him!"

Azalea looked like she was in shock and wouldn't say anything. Arnold leaned over toward me. "I tried, but every time I reach out to touch him, his girlfriend screams louder." As if to demonstrate, Arnold reached out toward the frozen guy, but sure enough, the woman screeched, "NO! Don't touch him! Nobody touch him until the ambulance gets here!"

My heart sank. "Ambulance?"

"Of course ambulance!" wailed the girlfriend.

"I called 911! This is an emergency!" She turned to the theater manager. "And when this is all over, there's going to be a massive lawsuit, I can tell you that much!" It appeared she wanted to take advantage of the situation to make sure poor Josh could become rich Josh.

The theater manager turned red, then started jabbering into her walkie-talkie. She was probably telling her bosses to call a good lawyer.

"We don't need an ambulance," I tried to tell the girlfriend. "Your friend was just Zombie Zing'd by accident. It's all a big misunderstanding. We can clear this up in two seconds if you just let my friend here take care of it."

"HANDS OFF!" she bellowed.

The rest of the audience had started to gather around to see what was going on. Some were taking videos with their cell phones.

Uh-oh.

Meanwhile, Ross and Kiki were on their phones, too, probably texting their parents.

Double uh-oh.

I knew I needed to let my mom know what was going on. But for some reason, I found myself physically unable to actually take my phone out of my pocket. Maybe I thought if I ignored it, everything would be fine. Maybe if

I closed my eyes, we could go back in time and this whole thing wouldn't have happened.

So I closed my eyes.

But then I opened them when I heard two people come charging up the aisle.

"The EMTs are here," the manager said into her walkie-talkie. "I'll keep you posted."

"What's an EMT?" I heard Arnold ask the manager.

"Emergency medical technicians," she told him. "They're going to get him into the ambulance and take him to the hospital so they can figure out what's wrong with this guy."

Triple uh-oh.

Ambulance?

HOSPITAL?

This was getting worse by the second. I had to tell them what was going on.

I ran up to one of the EMT people. "Excuse me? I can fix this!"

She barely looked at me. "Sorry, we're a little busy here."

"I know! But I can help! I can make him better!"

The EMT lady, who was helping set up a stretcher with the other guy, chuckled a little. "Is that right? What are you going to do, give him some of your sippy cup to make him feel all better?"

Well, that was rude. I suddenly got a little mad. And when I get a little mad, I get a little less shy. "No, I'm not. I'm trying to tell you that my friend is an afterlife human, and she gave this person the Zombie Zing by accident, since she was scared by the 3-D movie. The Zombie Zing paralyzes a person. And the only way to un-paralyze him is by un-zinging him. Which my other friend here can do, but nobody will let him."

The two EMTs looked at me. "Wait a second," said the other one, a man who for some reason was wearing a glove on only one of his hands. "You're saying this was a Zombie Zing?" He looked around. "I've heard about this. So who here is the zombie?"

Arnold raised his hand. Azalea was still a little too stunned to move, so I walked over to her and raised her hand for her.

"Two zombies!" said the guy EMT. He looked at his partner. "Well, this is our lucky day."

"EVERYONE STAND BACK!" hollered the woman EMT. "THERE ARE ZOMBIES IN OUR MIDST!"

"PLEASE DO NOT BE ALARMED!" added the other EMT, even though no one looked particularly alarmed.

I was confused. Hadn't these two gotten the memo that zombies weren't scary?

Kiki obviously thought the same thing. "Um, excuse me?" she said, tapping the EMT guy on the shoulder. "You don't need to be scaring people like that. They've been living peacefully and happily with us, and everyone knows that."

The guy nodded. "Sure, yeah, but in a medical emergency you can't be too careful." He leaned over to talk to Josh, who was still frozen in his seat. In all the commotion I'd almost forgotten he was there.

"WE'RE GONNA FIX THIS, BUDDY!" yelled the EMT, as if the paralysis had made Josh deaf.

Josh blinked his eyes twice, which may have meant *Thank you*. Or *Hurry up*.

The female EMT, who seemed to be a little less freaked out than the guy, looked back and forth between Azalea and Arnold. "So which one of you two put the hex on this guy?"

Before Azalea could even think about coming clean, Arnold raised his hand. "I did. The 3-D movie just got to me, I guess. I'd never seen one before."

"So you zapped this poor guy?" she said. "Then I advise you un-zap him."

"That's what I've been trying to tell you guys!" I
protested.

Josh's girlfriend seemed very unsure. "Wait a second,
you're going to let this zombie touch Josh again? What if
something even worse happens?"

"Everything will be fine," said the lady EMT. "We'll be
right here if something goes wrong!"

Josh's eyes widened when he heard the word *wrong*.

The lady EMT nodded at Arnold. "Go for it."

I crossed my fingers, and I'm pretty sure Kiki and

Ross did, too. Azalea just stood there. I think she'd decided she wasn't going to move until poor Josh could move.

Arnold didn't seem nervous at all, though. He just calmly walked up to Josh, put his hand on Josh's shoulder, and squeezed.

And just like that, Josh was fine. He yelled, "YES!" then raised his arms up like he'd just scored the winning touchdown in the Super Bowl. The crowd cheered, which made Josh even more psyched. First he hugged his girl-friend, who was expecting it, and then he hugged Arnold, who wasn't expecting it. The EMT guys started packing up their gear, and everything looked like it was going to be just fine. Which was when the two policemen showed up.

"We heard there was a Zombie Zing on an innocent bystander," said the first one.

The second one got out his notebook. "Tell us every-thing. Start at the beginning."

But before anyone could say anything, Azalea finally woke up out of her trance. "I did it!" she proclaimed. "I was watching the movie, and the 3-D scared me, and the creature was coming right toward me, and I thought I was being attacked, and I reached out to Zombie Zing him for my own protection, but instead I Zombie Zing'd the poor man sitting in front of me."

The EMTs looked confused. The guy pointed at Arnold. "I thought you said you did it."

Now Arnold *did* look nervous. "I . . . I was just trying to protect my friend."

"You don't need to protect me," Azalea said. "I don't belong here, and I never will. I'm starting to think this whole thing was a mistake."

She looked like she was going to cry, but then I remembered that Arnold told me zombies don't cry.

I walked over and put my arm around her. "You're being ridiculous. We love having you here! This was all just a big misunderstanding!"

The police and the EMTs stood there, trying to figure out what to do next. It seemed like everyone was waiting for someone else to do something, since no one had ever dealt with this kind of situation before. Then Josh—the guy who'd asked us to stop talking loudly, and then had been frozen solid for more than fifteen minutes, walked up to Azalea. I cringed—this wasn't going to be good.

"I totally understand what happened," he said. "It's okay. It's not your fault."

Azalea blinked. "Really?"

"Really. I was scared by the movie, too." The guy named Josh, who I'd thought I didn't like but now liked a lot, turned to the police and EMTs. "We're all good here, guys."

"But I need to file a report," one of the cops said.

"And I need to check you out fully before we give you a clean bill of health," one of the EMTs said.

"Fine. Let's go do it outside so everyone else can get back to the movie."

Josh went to go, but before he left, he turned to Azalea one last time. "Don't say you don't belong here. Give it another try. People can really surprise you sometimes."

He sure got that right.

STAYING ALIVE

After the *Floodthirsty* horror show—and I don't mean the movie—Azalea and I decided to lie low for a while. We had different reasons, though: She just wanted to stay out of the public eye while she got used to the idea of living among humans, and I wanted to hide in a dark corner because my hair was going to start falling out.

Yep. As in, I was going to be totally bald soon.

That's what happens when you get treatment for cancer. The good news is, it kills the cells that cause the disease. The bad news is, it also makes you lose your hair, your energy, and your appetite.

In the long term, it was a pretty fair trade-off.

But in the short term, I was going to look like ... well ... pick one:

a) a cue ball
b) an egghead

   c) Dr. Evil

   d) all of the above

One night at dinner, just as my hair was starting to fall out, my mom said, "Do you maybe want to try a wig?"

I looked at her like she was one of the monsters in *Floodthirsty*. "Uh, no. No wigs. I'd rather have no hair than look like an old man pretending to have hair."

"Fair enough," said my mom.

The next night at dinner, my mom said, "Do you want to go to the store and look at some hats?"

"Sure," I said.

Which was how I wound up with a new baseball hat of my favorite team (the Mets), a winter beanie that was "very hip-hop" (according to Darlene, who sold it to us), and something called a fedora, which was a hat that looked like the one Gene Kelly wears in *Singin' in the Rain,* which was my mom's favorite movie.

I pointed at the fedora. "I'm never gonna wear that."

"You say that now," she said. "But wait till the girls see you in it."

Slowly, I started to work the hats into my rotation at school, except for the fedora, of course. And also, I had to leave school at one o'clock three days a week to go for treatment at the hospital. When my hair started to fall out, everyone pretended not to notice, and the school let me wear my hats during class, which was usually against the rules. In general, people at school were super nice to me, and the people at the hospital were super nice to me, too, which made me feel a little better, but not so much better that I felt much like doing anything.

One night after dinner, Azalea said to me, "Arnold asked me today why you weren't sitting with him at lunch anymore."

"What did you tell him?"

"I said that you wanted to be alone because you weren't feeling well and also that you were a bit melancholy because your hair was going to fall out soon."

Sometimes I forget how honest zombies are.

"Oh," I said. "Well, I wish you hadn't said that."

"Why not?"

"Because it's embarrassing."

Azalea put down the book she was reading—she read around four books a week—and walked over to the couch where I was sitting, watching TV. "You should never be embarrassed," she said. "You should be proud of being such a fighter."

"I guess," I said.

"We're in this together, right?" Azalea smiled, which she didn't do all that often. "You and me. Trying to figure things out. But you can't do it alone, and neither can I."

I looked at Azalea. "Thanks," I said, trying to sound positive. It felt strange getting a pep talk from someone who had been raised in a laboratory and was trying to figure out how to survive in a world that had created her as an enemy, so I decided to change the subject. "How is the play going?"

"Oh, pretty good." Rehearsals for *Alice in Wonderland* had already started, and I'd heard that people were amazed how quickly Azalea had memorized the entire script. "We need some more people in the cast," she said. "Do you want to be in it?"

"Of course not," I said, more sharply than I meant to. "I've got more important things to do, like trying to stay alive."

I regretted it as soon as I said it, but it was too late. Azalea looked shocked, then immediately got up and went to her room. I wanted to go apologize to her, but for some reason I couldn't. I just wanted to be alone.

Like usual.

WE'RE HAIR FOR YOU

The next morning, my mom came in to wake me up for school, but I didn't want to go. First I pretended to be asleep, but when that didn't work, I mumbled, "I don't feel well."

"I know you don't feel well," my mom answered, "but that doesn't mean you can't go to school."

"Fine." I dragged myself out of bed, down the stairs, and to the kitchen table, where I moped my way through a bowl of cereal. Azalea, who was drinking a jelly bean smoothie, didn't say a word. It's possible she was too scared to start a conversation after I'd practically bitten her head off the night before.

My dad was sitting there reading his phone as usual. All of a sudden he looked up. "You know what I think, Ev? I think today is an excellent day for you to stop feeling sorry for yourself."

"Uh, what?" I said.

"You heard me. No more self-pity. We all take a few lumps in life. It's a lot easier to deal with if you fight your way through them with a good attitude."

I glared at him. "You don't have cancer, Dad."

"True," he said. "But I do have a son with cancer. So we're in this together. And instead of being sad or angry, I've decided to concentrate on the things I have to be grateful for. For example, I'm grateful for you."

"And I'm grateful for both of you," my mom said.

I glanced over at Azalea, who'd been listening quietly. I felt terrible, remembering how I'd snapped at her the night before. And I suddenly felt incredibly lucky just to be actually alive.

"I'm grateful for all of you," I said.

😵 😎 😃

The first clue I had that something was going to be different at school that day was when we pulled up to the parking lot. We were late leaving the house, because my mom couldn't find something, so we ended up getting to school about fifteen minutes after class started. Azalea jumped out of the car and ran inside without saying good-bye to my mom.

"Jeez, what's her rush?" I asked. "You called the

office and said we were going to be late, right?"

But my mom just smiled and said, "Have a great day!"

Then, when I walked up to the front door, I ran into a boy named Eddy Klompston. Eddy was famous for two things: He was the school pogo-jumping champion (apparently he pogo-jumped for three hours and forty-seven minutes without falling), and he had a giant mop of red curly hair.

As far as I knew, he was still the pogo-jumping champion, but the giant mop of red curly hair was gone. In fact, *all* of his red curly hair was gone.

Yup. He was totally bald.

"Uh, Eddy?" I asked.

He barely glanced at me. "Oh, hey, Evan, what's up?"

"You, uh . . . you . . ." I pointed to the top of his head.

"Oh, you mean my hair? Yeah, I decided to cut it off. You know, just felt like the right move. Anyway, I'm late!" He waved slightly, then headed inside. I followed him into the office, where late students had to check in. That's when I noticed the next weird thing—everyone was smiling in this kind of strange way. Even Betsy, the woman at the front office desk who was usually incredibly chatty, wasn't saying much. When I handed her my note, she just smiled and said, "You may proceed to class, Evan."

So I did.

I walked down the hall and noticed it was quiet. Really, really quiet. When I got to the sixth-grade wing, I peered into a few classrooms and noticed they were empty.

I thought to myself, *Where is everybody?*

Then I got to my classroom, and there was a note on the door:

Evan, Please report to the Gymnasium.
Mrs. HuGGle

Things were just getting stranger. We never had gym first thing in the morning! But there was no one around to ask, so I headed down to the gym.

I pushed the door open, and the first person I saw was Coach Hank.

Who was also bald.

"Coach Hank, you're bald," I said, pointing out something I was pretty sure he already knew.

He just laughed and said, "Come on in!" in that incredibly loud and overexcited voice he had. So I went in, and I saw about sixty kids sitting on the bleachers.

Almost all of them were bald, too.

And slowly…slowly…it started to dawn on me what was happening.

My friends…actually a lot more people than just my friends…had all cut their hair off.

All of it.

For *me*.

I walked over to where they were all sitting and smiling. In the front row, Arnold and Azalea were next to each other. They were both bald. Azalea must have run inside after getting out of the car, and somebody must have shaved her head in, like, five minutes!

I looked around. There was Ross, and Kiki, and Brett, and Callie, and James, and Geneva, and Cedric, and everyone else, and they all had no hair.

It was the strangest thing I'd ever seen.

And the most awesome.

Arnold got up. "Hey," he said.

"Hey," I said.

Arnold stood there awkwardly for a second, looking a little nervous. Then Coach Hank handed him a microphone, and I realized why: He was about to make a speech.

Arnold cleared his throat for a second. "Um, hi, everyone," he said, his soft voice echoing around the

gymnasium. "Thanks for coming." He turned to look at me. "So, uh, you might have noticed something different about us." Everyone laughed, which seemed to relax Arnold a bit. "Yup, we all cut our hair off. We figured, why did you get to be the only one who looked totally cool with no hair? That didn't seem fair, and we wanted in on the action."

Then Kiki came up to the microphone. "And also, we're happy to say that we donated all our hair to an organization called We're Hair for You, which creates wigs for people with cancer and other diseases that cause their hair to fall out."

Kiki sat back down. Then my teacher, Mrs. Huggle, came up to the microphone. She hadn't cut her hair off, but she had a big smile on her face. "I would just like to add," she said, "that this is one of the most special things I've ever seen here in my many years at Bernard J. Frumpstein Elementary School. And I would like to thank the student who had the idea in the first place. And I would also like him to stand up so he might be acknowledged."

When I heard her say *him*, I was surprised because I had been sure that it was Kiki's idea. Then I realized that it must have been Arnold, and I was about to thank him, but then I realized he was already standing up, so it couldn't have been him either.

Huh?

I was trying to figure out who it could be when I saw Ross Klepsaw stand up. I figured he must have just been stretching or something, but nope. He was smiling, and then everybody started to clap, and then he waved at all the clapping people, and that was when I realized: *Holy smokes. This whole thing was Ross Klepsaw's idea.*

Actually, it was more like, *HOLY SMOKES! THIS WHOLE THING WAS ROSS KLEPSAW'S IDEA?!?!?!?!?*

I walked over to him. "You did this for me?"

"Dude!" he said, which wasn't surprising, since it was his favorite word. "Uh, yeah, I guess I did. I mean, I feel bad because I wasn't really all that nice to you for years, you know? I was kind of a jerk, to be honest. So then, you know, when your whole cancer thing came back, I made up my mind that I was going to be a lot nicer. And then when you started losing your hair and stuff, I guess that's when I thought of the idea that maybe, if we all cut off our hair, too, you wouldn't have to feel, like, you know... alone, I guess."

"Wow," I said. "That is ..." But I didn't have the words to finish the sentence. Instead, I looked over at Kiki and said, "I'm sorry if I made you feel bad about liking Ross. I guess you knew something I didn't."

She laughed. "I didn't! I thought he was just as obnoxious as you did!"

"Hey," Ross said, but he didn't sound mad.

Kiki put her arm around Ross's shoulder. "I did know there was something about him, I guess. Even if he didn't know it himself."

And as I watched them smile at each other—bald

boyfriend and bald girlfriend—I didn't feel jealous, or irritated, or left out. I actually felt something I hadn't felt in a pretty long time.

Happy.

FEELING BLUE

Scientific data has proven beyond a doubt that there are very few things more odd-looking than a sixth-grade zombie girl.

But one could surmise that one of those things is probably a sixth-grade zombie girl who is bald.

And another one of those things is *definitely* a sixth-grade zombie girl with blue hair.

I should know.

I've been all three of those things.

On that morning, I'd done exactly what Arnold Z. Ombee had asked me to do, and what Mr. and Mrs. Brantley had said was okay to do: gone to the nurse's office, where Nurse Raposo—who was very nice, by the way—proceeded to shave my head in about ten seconds flat.

I hadn't mentioned a word about it to Evan, because

it was a secret. The surprise worked extremely well: When Evan walked into the gymnasium full of bald boys—and some bald girls, too—he was shocked. It was the happiest I'd seen him since I'd moved into their house.

For the next several weeks, a bunch of the other children stayed bald, because they said they weren't going to grow their hair back until Evan's treatment was completed. Other children decided to grow their hair back. I wasn't sure what I was going to do, but a few days after I cut my hair, I was reading a book at the kitchen table when Mrs. Brantley said to me, "Azalea, have you been experimenting with hair products?"

"What's a hair product?" I asked her.

She laughed slightly. "Well, hon, it's something that does something to your hair. Like makes it look wet, for example, or makes it stay in place on a windy day. And sometimes it makes hair change color. And as your hair is coming in blue, I was wondering if Lester Kinder's friend Darlene had lent you some product."

"I'm sorry, did you say blue?"

"Why, yes. Haven't you checked the mirror recently?"

That was an unnecessary question. I never checked the mirror. I could not comprehend why regular humans did it all the time. Didn't they already know what they looked like? They lived with themselves twenty-four hours a day.

"I'm sorry, I have not."

"Well, you might want to, hon."

"Very well." I went to the downstairs bathroom and looked in the mirror. It was always strange to look at myself, but it was stranger today, because Mrs. Brantley was correct: My hair—which at that point was still very short and bristly—was coming in light blue.

I touched it, just to make sure it was really there—I

was still finding it hard to trust mirrors—and confirmed that it was. Then I went back to the kitchen table.

"My hair is blue," I said to Mrs. Brantley, even though she'd been the one to tell me that in the first place.

"I guess that wasn't in the zombie handbook," she said. I knew she was trying to make a joke, so I tried to laugh.

Just then, Evan came in from taking out the garbage. "Hey, everyone, what's going on?"

"My hair is blue," I repeated.

"Huh?" He walked over to me to get a closer look. "Holy smokes, it is," he said. "That is so cool!" He took out his phone. "I gotta tell Arnold, so he can tell Lester, so he can tell Darlene. She's gonna love this!"

Evan called Arnold's house and put the phone on speaker so we could all hear.

"Hello?" said a voice, probably Arnold's mother.

"Hi, Mrs. Kinder," Evan said. "Is Arnold there?"

"Oh, hi, Evan! Of course, just hold on a sec. We're having some drama over here at the moment."

"What kind of drama?" Evan asked, but Mrs. Kinder was already gone.

Two seconds later, Arnold came on the phone. "Evan! Guess what?"

"What?"

"My hair is turning blue!"

We all looked at one another. "That's pretty funny," Evan told Arnold, "because so is Azalea's."

So that's how we discovered that when you cut off an afterlife human's hair, it grows back blue. Darlene was so excited that she wrote a whole blog post about it. She took pictures of Arnold and me once a week, and pretty soon the whole town was following how our hair was growing. Then the next thing we knew, people started showing up at school with blue hair—at first, just a few, but pretty soon it was more than half the students in our grade.

Then Coach Hank came in with blue hair. Coach Hank was a very odd person.

During all of the blue-hair commotion, the last thing anybody cared about or noticed was the fact that Evan's hair had now completely fallen out. Even Evan himself didn't care.

So I guess my hair turned blue for a reason.

dOWN THE RABBIT HOLE

"'Curiouser and curiouser'?" I asked Mrs. Huggle. "That's not proper English, is it?"

She sighed. "You're correct, Azalea. Technically it's not proper English. However, since it's one of the most famous things Alice says, and since you're playing Alice, and since the play we're doing is *Alice in Wonderland*, I'm going to have to ask you to say the line anyway."

"Why is that line so famous if it's not proper English?" I asked.

Mrs. Huggle sighed again.

I asked Mrs. Huggle a lot of questions.

Fortunately, she was a very patient person.

😣 😎 😋

My brain works differently from regular humans'. I think most regular humans accept things that don't make sense, as long as everyone else accepts them. But if something doesn't make sense to me, I will ask why.

Over and over again.

😖 😎 😄

The other children who were in the play rolled their eyes every time I asked a question, but I couldn't help it. And they knew they couldn't blame me, anyway—I was created that way.

"Okay, Mrs. Huggle," I said. "I will say 'curiouser and curiouser.' I don't understand it, but I will say it."

We had been rehearsing the play for seventeen days, and the performance was the next night. Apparently a lot of people were going to attend the play. Evan said it was "kind of a big deal." But I didn't know what that meant until we pulled into the school parking lot the night of the performance, and every space was filled. There were even cars parked alongside the road. I had never seen that before.

"Wow," said Mr. Brantley, "this place is packed."

As we walked inside, I started to get this feeling in my stomach that I didn't recognize. It was a tumultuous feeling, almost as if I'd eaten too many jelly beans for dinner. But I hadn't. I'd only eaten eighteen. (I always counted.)

Evan looked at me. "Hey, are you okay? You look a little . . . I don't know . . . off."

Mrs. Brantley glanced back at me. "He's right," she said. "You look even paler than usual. Maybe a little bit of stage fright is kicking in?"

"Stage fright?" I asked. "What's that?"

"Uh, well..." Mrs. Brantley trailed off. She looked like she regretted bringing it up in the first place.

But Evan was happy to fill in. "Stage fright is when you're about to go on a stage to perform in front of a lot of people, but then you get so nervous you can't do it."

"I'm pretty sure afterlife humans would not experience stage fright in the same way that normal humans would," said Mr. Brantley, but it was too late— the damage was done.

I officially had stage fright, and plenty of it.

I went into the auditorium, which was already half full,

even though the show wasn't for another thirty minutes. Mrs. Huggle, who was scurrying around trying to get everything organized, saw me and came running over. "Azalea! We need to get you into costume right away!" She took me by the hand and led me over to a table in front of a big mirror. All these mirrors! I looked at myself again. My blue hair was coming in more thickly now. I was going to be a blue-haired Alice. In front of a lot of people I didn't know. What if they all laughed at me? What if they all thought I looked ridiculous? What if I tripped over the scenery and fell on my face?

My stage fright was asking a lot of questions.

Kiki, who was sitting next to me, putting her costume on, noticed how nervous I seemed. "Hey, are you okay?" she asked.

"I have no idea," I said honestly. Then I had an idea. "Hey, do you want to play Alice? Everyone says you usually play the lead roles in the plays."

She shrugged. "Well, yeah, I guess that's true, but you're gonna kill it."

I frowned. "'Kill it'? That sounds terrible."

She let out a loud laugh. "Ha! No, 'kill it' is good. It means be awesome." Then she thought for a second. "I can see how being in a play for the first time would

confuse someone, though, because there are a lot of expressions that sound bad but actually mean something good. Like 'kill it.' 'Knock 'em dead.' 'Break a leg.'"

"'Break a leg'? What does that mean?"

"It means good luck," Kiki said. "But you don't need any luck, because you're gonna be great."

"Thanks," I said. "And I hope you break a leg, too."

That made her crack up, and suddenly I felt better.

Kiki was like that.

After I hurried into my Alice outfit, I went to the side

of the stage and peeked out from behind the curtain. The auditorium was practically full! I scanned the audience, looking for people I knew, which turned out to be not very many. Then I saw somebody who at first I thought I didn't recognize, and then realized I did.

Dr. Grasmere was there.

The doctor from the Territory, who had surprised us at dinner that night a few months ago. The doctor who had tried to trap and trick Arnold when he'd come back to help. The doctor who said he wasn't working on Project Z anymore but would be "keeping an eye on things," anyway. He was there in his red jacket, sitting by himself in the third row, reading his program and smiling.

A cold shiver ran through my body. The stage fright was now replaced by a more general fright.

"Places, everyone!" cried Mrs. Huggle. "We're about to begin! Places, please—and good luck to all!"

I took my position on the stage. The lights went dark and the audience hushed. All the rehearsing we'd done had led up to this moment. But all I could think about was Dr. Grasmere, sitting there, probably trying to fig-ure out a way to ruin everything.

There was a buzzing in my ears, kind of like the buzz-ing they used in the Territory when they were in the middle of programming our brains. Francesca Wormser, who was playing the narrator, was moving her lips, but I couldn't hear the words she was saying. I glanced out at Dr. Grasmere. His smile was wider. I looked at Mrs. Huggle, who was off to the side of the stage, pacing anxiously. She saw me and gave me a thumbs-up, but it didn't help. The buzzing in my head got louder, so I moved closer to Francesca, until finally I could make out the words she was saying.

"And so she went down the rabbit hole!"

A small part of my brain realized that was my cue to start speaking, but the rest of my brain couldn't remember what I was supposed to say.

"DOWN THE RABBIT HOLE!" said Francesca again, louder and more insistent this time.

Mrs. Huggle rushed out onto the stage. "*What a wonderful adventure I'm about to have,*" she said, so quietly only I could hear it.

"What kind of adventure?" I asked her.

"No, dear, that's your line," she said. "You can do it. I know you can."

Dr. Grasmere was still staring up at me, waiting for me to fail. But Mrs. Huggle, with her kind eyes, was encouraging me to succeed.

And somehow, I managed to listen to the part of my brain that told me to listen more to Mrs. Huggle than Dr. Grasmere.

I turned out to the audience. "WHAT A WONDERFUL ADVENTURE I'M ABOUT TO HAVE!" I said, as loud as I possibly could.

Everyone started clapping and cheering. I smiled, and it felt like a giant weight was lifted off my shoulders.

The rest of the play went great. I remembered every line, and at the end we got a standing ovation.

Curiouser and curiouser, indeed.

SPECIAL dELIVERY

After the play ended, we got our standing ovation and took our bows. Then we went backstage and hugged and congratulated one another and changed back into our regular clothes. Then we went out to the lobby, where people were waiting to say incredibly nice things to us.

It was the strangest feeling. People were shouting stuff like "You were great!" and "How did you memorize all those lines!" and "You were born to play Alice!" (I could have corrected that person by reminding them that I'd never actually been born, but it didn't seem like the right time or place for that.) Some people were hugging me like they knew me, even though they didn't.

Like I said, it was strange.

Evan and his parents were waiting for me by the refreshments. When they saw me coming, they all clapped.

"Watch out, Broadway, here she comes!" Evan cried.

I wasn't sure what Broadway was, but I was pretty sure Evan was giving me a compliment, so I said, "Thank you."

We chatted about the show for about five minutes, and I was telling them how Mrs. Huggle helped me at the beginning when Mr. Brantley said, "Did you see who was here?"

I nodded. "Yes, I saw Dr. Grasmere. Did you know he was coming?"

"I had no idea," Mr. Brantley said. "And I'm sure his presence made you even more nervous than you were already."

"It did," I admitted.

"Well, you acquitted yourself wonderfully well; we're all so proud of you," said Mrs. Brantley.

"That's for sure!" added Evan.

"Dr. Grasmere couldn't stay after," said Mr. Brantley, "but he wanted me to congratulate you on his behalf. He thought your performance was very strong." He reached into his jacket pocket and took out an envelope. "But the other reason he came tonight was to give you this letter. Apparently it's from two of your fellow residents in the Territory, and they were able to get the letter to you with Dr. Grasmere's help."

"I don't understand," I said. "Who is Dr. Grasmere trying to help? And why? He was always against us."

Mr. Brantley shrugged. "Not sure. It's addressed to you, so I wasn't going to open it."

I took the letter and stuffed it into my pocket. "Thank you," I said.

Evan looked surprised. "Don't you want to read it?"

I did, of course, very much. But for some reason I decided that a hallway full of screaming and happy people was probably not the best place to do that. "I will look at it later."

"That makes sense," said Mrs. Brantley. "Tonight is for celebrating! Let's have some punch!"

There was a big bowl of jelly beans—put out for me, of course, and I guess for Arnold, too—and I helped myself to a handful. Kiki and Ross spotted me and came running over.

"That was awesome!" Kiki said.

Ross looked a little shy. I'd never seen him look shy before. "How did you memorize all those words?" he asked. "I would never be able to do that."

"Yes, you would," I told him. "Believe it or not, you can do all sorts of things you didn't know you could do."

"Says you," he said, picking out ten red jelly beans

and popping them into his mouth all at once.

Sarah Anne came over, too, with someone who was probably her dad. She was a very interesting person: She was really smart, you could tell, but she was very specific about how she communicated with people. She talked by pointing at letters on a board, and she wasn't comfortable looking directly at anyone.

At first, I'd struggled to understand her, because she pointed at letters so fast, but over the last few weeks I was starting to figure it out.

YOU WERE REALLY GOOD TONIGHT, she said. YOU MAKE A GREAT ALICE. JUST RIGHT FOR THE PART.

"Thanks," I said. "What do you mean, 'right for the part'?"

Sarah Anne hesitated for a few seconds, then started pointing again. ALICE IS BRAVE BECAUSE SHE IS WILLING TO GO TO A STRANGE PLACE TO HAVE AN ADVENTURE, she said. JUST LIKE YOU.

"I guess you're right," I said. "But I think she might be a little more brave than I am."

"What are you guys talking about?" asked Arnold, who had just walked over.

"Oh, not much," I told him. "Sarah Anne was just saying how Alice and I have a lot in common, and I was just saying how Alice had a lot more courage than I had."

Arnold laughed. "That's ridiculous."

TOTALLY RIDICULOUS, Sarah Anne said.

I glanced around the room to make sure no one else was listening. "May I say something confidentially? I was almost unable to perform tonight because Dr. Grasmere was here."

Arnold's face went even whiter than it already was. "What? He was? I didn't see him. And I'm glad I didn't."

"Yes, he was sitting right in the third row." I took

out the envelope. "And he brought me a letter from someone inside the Territory."

Arnold and Sarah Anne looked at each other, then Sarah Anne decided to ask the obvious question.

ARE YOU GOING TO READ IT?

I nodded. "Tonight, when I get home."

I know Arnold and Sarah Anne were both dying to know who'd sent the letter, and what it said. So was I. But I put it back in my pocket, and neither of them asked me about it again.

Good friends know when to give you support, but they also know when to leave you alone.

A REPORT FROM INSIDE

After about an hour of celebrating, taking pictures, and many people telling me I should become a professional actor (I tried to laugh politely), we headed home. The Brantleys knew I wanted to read the letter as quickly as possible, so they left me alone as I went into the living room, sat on the love seat (I don't understand why they call it that, by the way), turned on the lamp, and opened the envelope.

Dear Azalea:

We hope you have been doing well in your new home. We think of you often, and we miss you.

We don't have very much to report in the way of news, but there is a general feeling of unease around the campus. Commander Jensen is not around very much anymore, and people are wondering why. The soldiers seem to be acting differently, too. There is a lot of huddling in corners, and whispering, and they seem to be less concerned with our training. It is almost as if the regular humans don't care as much about the afterlife humans as they used to. That isn't necessarily a bad thing, because all that training and lecturing was a bit wearying, as you know—but at the same time, it could mean that significant changes are being planned.

One unusual thing has happened, however: Dr. Grasmere has reappeared here in the Territory several times over the last few weeks. He made an announcement at dinner one night and said he is working on a few projects. Everyone is concerned, because as you may recall, he was not kind to the subjects. However, he has made a significant effort to be more benevolent this time. In fact, it was his idea to have us write you a letter, which he himself promised he would deliver. If you are reading this now, that means he kept his promise—so maybe he has become friendlier after all!

Well, that is probably enough for now. We have never written a letter to anyone before, so we have no idea how long they are supposed to be, but it seems we have said all we have to say. Let us just reiterate how much we miss you, and how hopeful we are that you are doing well. Your success is our success! And we are so happy for you.

Your friends,

Berstus and Frumpus Clacknozzle

Wow.

Berstus and Frumpus had been my podmates, meaning I'd lived with them. I was closer to them than I was to any other afterlife humans. Hearing their voices— if only in my head—was a shock.

I put the piece of paper down and closed my eyes. I tried to remember what life was like back in the Territory, but it was hard. Our memories are programmed in a very peculiar fashion. Some things we remember very well (like all of Alice's lines in *Alice in Wonderland*), but other things are very foggy (like the entire past). I concentrated extremely hard, and fragments of images finally appeared in my head—the wooden bench I used to lie on in my pod, and the sad smile on Frumpus's face when he waved good-bye to me for the last time—but overall it was frustratingly vague. What wasn't vague, however, was Berstus's and Frumpus's attitude in the letter.

They were scared.

And I had no way to help them.

I went back into the kitchen, where Mr. and Mrs. Brantley were sitting at the table. Evan was in the family room, watching television, which was good. I didn't really want him to hear what I was about to say.

"Well?" said Mrs. Brantley. "Who was it from, and what did it say?"

"It was from Berstus and Frumpus, my friends from the Territory." I hesitated before going on.

"Is everything all right?" asked Mr. Brantley.

"I don't know," I answered. "At first, they said there wasn't much news to report. But then by the end of the letter it sounded like they were scared."

Mrs. Brantley frowned. "About what?"

"I don't know, exactly." Mr. Brantley pushed the bowl of jelly beans in my direction, and I took a handful. "I guess they feel like something is about to happen— something bad—and the people in charge aren't telling them what's going on."

"That seems odd," Mr. Brantley said. "Commander Jensen seemed so committed to the assimilation program. Maybe there have been some decisions made that we don't know about. I'll make a call and try to find out what's going on."

"I would appreciate that," I told him.

But there was something I didn't tell him, or Mrs. Brantley, or Evan, or anyone else that night.

I had made a decision of my own.

THE FIRST SWEAT

I know you have heard about zombie sweat, so I will spare you the terribly embarrassing details about what it looks like (slimy), what color it is (yellow), what it smells like (rotten eggs times a thousand), and what happens when regular humans see it (they get very upset).

But what I will tell you is that the next day in gym, I sweated in front of humans for the first time.

I know, it sounds difficult to believe, right? How could I have not sweated when I was about to perform the role of Alice in *Alice in Wonderland* in front of the whole school, with Dr. Grasmere staring at me from the third row? And then on top of that, I forgot my lines? But for some reason, I didn't sweat. Remember, zombies only sweat when we're nervous. So maybe I wasn't nervous. Maybe I was way past nervous that night, and had gone straight to terrified.

In any event, I didn't sweat that night. But in gym

class, while looking at Eric Dasher (who was a very nice human boy), and after having heard the words he'd spoken ("Would you consider sitting next to me at the graduation ceremony next month?"), I felt my sneakers starting to get a little squishy.

Gloop. Gloop. Squish. Squish.

I started backing up slowly, trying to ease my way out of odor range. "I'm terribly sorry, but what did you say?"

But Eric, unfortunately, was stepping toward me as fast as I was stepping away from him. "I was just thinking, you seem really nice, and maybe it would be cool if we could hang out at graduation, you know, by sitting together, and hanging out and stuff."

"Oh. Well, that certainly is a nice offer, and I will consider it."

Eric laughed. "Do you have to be so formal about it?" Then he suddenly stopped talking. I was quite sure I knew why. "Uh, hey, do you smell that?"

"Smell what?"

He wrinkled his nose. "I don't know...uh...*that*. It's...I mean...whoa. It's really *gross*."

"I'm not sure I know what you're referring to," I said, which was the exact moment I discovered that afterlife humans could lie. Living among regular humans had made me realize that sometimes the truth was a very difficult thing to say.

In the meantime, other kids started picking up the scent. "What *is that*?" someone said, while various moans and groans were heard throughout the gymnasium. But then Ross Klepsaw came running over and put an end to the mystery.

"I know *exactly* what that is!" He thrust his finger down in the direction of my sneakers. "Look! Zombie sweat! I recognize that stink anywhere!"

I looked sadly at Ross, wondering what had happened to the boy who'd convinced every kid in the school to cut their hair off.

The smell of zombie sweat put an end to all that, I guess.

A collective "Ewwwwwww!" rang in my ears, from essentially the entire gym class.

Arnold tried to help me out. "Guys, remember when I got the zombie sweats? It happens! I'll take Azalea to the nurse's office, and we'll get her cleaned up. Please don't make her feel bad!"

As Arnold and I walked out of the gym, I heard two boys I didn't know whispering to each other.

"What did people expect?" said one of the boys. "These zombies can never fit in. I mean, come on, we've all seen the movies! They're more like monsters than people!"

The other boy laughed. "Totally! But there was nothing in the zombie movies about that incredibly stinky sweat! I mean, that's even scarier than eating brains and stuff!"

They both laughed.

"Shut up, you guys," said Arnold, while I pretended I didn't hear them. I was too busy glancing back at Eric Dasher. He was talking to one of his friends, pointing at his feet and laughing. I was pretty sure he was making fun of me, too.

I guess the whole sitting-next-to-each-other-at-graduation thing was off.

WoRd 9ETs OuT

When we got to her office, Nurse Raposo was attending to a child whose poison ivy rash was acting up.

"My two favorite afterlifes!" she cried, which was funny, since I'm pretty sure we were the only two afterlifes she knew. "What can I do for you?"

I was still too embarrassed to say anything, so Arnold spoke up. "Azalea had a small incident. She excreted some zombie sweat in gym, and let's just say it pretty much brought things to a grinding halt."

Nurse Raposo nodded and looked at me with a gentle smile. "Well, let's see what we can do about that. Would you mind taking your shoes off, dear?"

Actually, I did mind. Taking my shoes off meant exposing everyone to more zombie sweat, which was probably caked to my socks. I wasn't sure how that would help anything.

"Don't you worry about a thing," the nurse added,

even though she clearly knew I was worried about many things. "I've seen way worse."

I did as I was told and removed my shoes. The nurse immediately took them and placed them in the sink and ran hot water over them. I took my socks off and she threw them in a trash can with a lid. Then she went into a closet, retrieved a brand-new pair of socks and a pair of sandals, and offered them to me. "These should get you through the rest of the day."

I looked at her for a second. "Can I lie down for a minute?"

"Sure." She patted one of the two cots that were in her office. "Please avail yourself of one of my comfy cozy master bedroom suites."

She was making a joke, of course, but I didn't have the energy to laugh. I lay down on the cot and considered everything that had happened to me since I tried to fit into the real world:

I Zombie Zing'd a complete stranger.

I Zombie Sweat'd a classmate.

I performed in the school play, but not before I had a full-blown panic attack.

I got a letter from my podmates in the Territory saying they felt like something bad was about to happen.

I heard students talking about me like I was some sort of monster.

Nurse Raposo interrupted my train of thought. "Are you comfortable, Azalea? Would you like some water?" She pulled up a chair and smiled kindly. "When do you think you'll be ready to return to class?"

I tried to smile back, but I couldn't, so instead I just closed my eyes. I didn't have the heart to tell her what my real answers were.

Am I comfortable?

No.

When will I feel ready to return to class?

Never.

Ready or not, I went back to class about twenty minutes later, but pretty much kept to myself straight through lunch. Then, at recess, when everyone headed over to the fields to play games, or the jungle gym to climb around, I went and sat by myself on a bench. I didn't feel much like playing or climbing.

But I wasn't by myself for long, because five minutes later Sarah Anne came over to join me.

WHAT ARE YOU DOING ON MY BENCH? she asked.

I shrugged. "Not much, I guess."

OKAY. DO YOU MIND IF I SIT HERE, TOO?

"Of course not."

GREAT.

She opened up her book.

"What are you reading?"

She showed me the cover. *Animal Poems, 1800–2000.*

"Wow, that sounds cool."

IT IS, she said.

I let her read in peace for about five minutes, and then I heard myself say, "I'm going back to the Territory."

She looked at me, which was unusual, since she rarely looked directly at anybody. WHAT DO YOU MEAN?

"I mean, I don't think I should stay here anymore. I don't think I belong here. So I'm going to go back where I belong."

Sarah Anne put her book down, grabbed her letter board, then got up and ran off. I wondered what she was doing until I saw her approach Arnold, Evan, Ross, and Kiki, point at her letter board, and point over at me. They all started running in my direction.

I guess there was no turning back now.

Kiki was the first to reach me. "What is going on?" she demanded. "You're talking about going back to the Territory? For real?"

"Is this because of the zombie sweat?" Ross added. "I mean, yeah, that stuff is gross, everybody knows that, but so what? I mean, it's not worth giving up on this whole thing, you know?"

I wasn't sure what to say to them, so I didn't say anything.

By then, Arnold and Evan, the two slowest of the

bunch, had reached the bench, too. Evan was a little out of breath, but Arnold said, "We need to talk about this. Please."

"I'm not sure we do," I said. "Arnold, you are doing great here, and that's wonderful. But that doesn't mean that it's right for everyone. And I've decided it's not right for me."

"Why?" asked Ross. "Why would you want to go back there? Isn't it, like, basically a jail?"

I wasn't really sure how to answer that. "I know it seems like that, but it's really the only home I've ever known. And in a way, being out here"—I held my arms out, to indicate the world in general—"being out here is like a jail to me. Because I don't feel free. I feel like I'm being watched all the time, and I have to act in a certain way, and there's a lot of pressure on me, and I don't think I can handle it for very much longer." I hesitated for a second. "And also, I heard from my pod-mates Berstus and Frumpus. They wrote me that something is different, and Commander Jensen isn't there very much, and it feels like big changes are about to happen, and they're scared, and it made me want to go be with them."

Kiki sat down next to me on the bench. "This is

crazy," she said. "You're going to leave now, right before we graduate?"

"What if my parents and I go meet with Commander Jensen to find out what's really going on?" Arnold said. "Would that help?"

"I don't know," I said. "It didn't seem like he was involved that much anymore."

"We'll find out," Arnold insisted. "I'll have my parents arrange a visit."

Finally, Evan had regained his breath and was ready to talk. "I have something to say," he said.

Everyone stopped chattering.

"I have my last chemotherapy treatment next week," he said. "And I was planning on having a party to celebrate that, and our graduation. Azalea, I would like very much for you to agree to stay at least until then. Please."

All eyes were on me. "I—I don't know," I said. "I really appreciate how nice you are all being to me. I promise to think about it."

Sarah Anne, who had been quiet while everyone else was chattering, took out her letter board.

THEN IT'S SETTLED, she said. SHE'S STAYING. AT LEAST FOR NOW.

A NOBLE EXPERIMENT

I could tell something was different as soon as I saw Sergeant Kelly.

She was waiting there when my parents and I drove up to Commander Jensen's headquarters. But instead of her usual bright smile and helpful attitude, she looked like she was all business.

"Good afternoon, Dr. and Mr. Kinder," she said formally. "Good afternoon to you as well, Arnold."

"Good afternoon?" I said. "Okay, then, good afternoon it is."

She nodded without smiling.

"How have you been, Sergeant?" asked my mom. "Are you well?"

"Very well, ma'am, thank you for asking."

My mom arched her eyebrows in surprise. "'Ma'am'?"

But Sergeant Kelly didn't seem to get the joke. "I will alert Commander Jensen that you're here."

As she walked away, my parents looked at each other. "Jeez," said my dad. "No funny business with her today, huh?"

My mom shook her head. "It's like she had no idea who we were."

"Or didn't want to know," my dad responded.

After five minutes, Sergeant Kelly came back. "The commander would like me to escort you to his office."

"Thank you, Sergeant Kelly," said my dad, adopting her serious and formal tone. We walked down the long hall that I remembered from the last time we were at the compound. The walls were lined with pictures of the commander with many different people, none of whom I recognized. But my mom pointed at one or two and whistled, like she was impressed.

"Who is that woman?" I asked, after one such whistle.

"Oh, no one too important," she said, in not much more than a whisper. "Just the president of the United States."

It was my turn to whistle.

Finally we turned into Commander Jensen's office. Sergeant Kelly motioned for us to take a seat, then headed out of the room. But before she left, she turned back quickly.

"It's very good to see you all again," she said. "Take care."

But before any of us had a chance to say the same to her, she was gone.

Commander Jensen was finishing up a phone call, so we waited quietly.

"I don't want to break protocol," he was saying into the phone. "And I don't want to hear it from Colonel Brisco; he has no authority in this matter. If Sherman has been put in charge, then that's fine, but I need to hear it from someone higher up the chain of command. Until that happens, we have nothing further to discuss."

My parents and I looked at each other. *Sherman.*

That was Dr. Grasmere's first name.

Commander Jensen hung up the phone, then got up and came around his desk to shake hands with all of us. "Well, how's that for timing?" he said, with a slight smile on his face. "I'm sure I can guess why you're here, and as you just heard, we're smack in the middle of sorting out some stuff here."

My dad got right to the point. "What kind of stuff?"

"Well, stuff that's a little complicated, to be honest with you." Commander Jensen sat back down behind his giant desk, which kind of looked like a spaceship that was about to take off. "There's not a lot I can talk about right now. Things are still being worked out, and I'm sure you can understand that we're operating with strict confidentiality protocols."

"Jon," said my mom. Her voice was as firm and steady as I'd ever heard it. "We've known each other a long time. A very long time. I know you can't tell us everything, but I would expect the common courtesy of some basic information."

I raised my hand like I was in school for some reason.

"Azalea received a letter from her podmates, Berstus and Frumpus Clacknozzle. She said they seemed very worried."

Commander Jensen took a deep breath. "I heard about that. That wasn't supposed to happen. There was a breach that I've discussed with Dr. Grasmere."

"Well, it's got my son concerned as well," said my dad. "And when he's concerned, we're concerned."

Commander Jensen opened a folder that was on his desk. It reminded me of Dr. Grasmere, who always carried a red folder around, back when I was in the Territory. Nothing good had ever happened when Dr. Grasmere was looking in his red folder.

At least Commander Jensen's folder was blue.

He shuffled a few papers until he found the one he was looking for. "Here we go," he said. "This is about as much as I can tell you." He put on his reading glasses and quietly cleared his throat. "*Due to a variety of circumstances which have been detailed in a series of previous memos, the U.S. Martial Services has been directed to initiate a Cease Operations Order of the Human Reanimation Program, otherwise known as Project Z, which originated under Proclamation 358249-A, dated July 19, 2024. This COO is to be initiated immediately. No additional subjects will be developed, and all existing subjects will be removed to an undisclosed location TBD. As of now, future plans for these subjects remain an open question. It is hoped that they will be used for further research that will enhance the study of medicine and human anatomy.*" Commander Jensen stopped reading and removed his glasses. "As I said, that's all I can tell you."

"I'm not sure I understand," I said, which was more hopeful than true. I was pretty sure I understood perfectly.

My mom looked at me with sadness in her eyes. "It's over," she said. "Project Z is over."

"Isn't this what you wanted, Jenny?" asked Commander Jensen. "You never fully supported what was happening here. And now, at last, it appears that the U.S. government agrees with you."

My mom flashed her eyes at the commander. "I never fully supported the program? That's true. I never supported exploiting the afterlife humans and sending them into battle like they were robots. But I also don't support randomly shutting the program down without a plan to take care of them."

"I never said there wasn't a plan." The commander rubbed his face, and I suddenly realized how tired he looked. "And for the record, I don't support what's happening here either. That's why they've scaled back my involvement in the assignment. It's back in Dr. Grasmere's jurisdiction now."

"Where are the afterlifes being sent?" asked my dad. "You must know at least that much."

Commander Jensen sighed. "I heard something about an island off the coast of Maine. They're repurposing an old abandoned military outpost."

"Maine?" exclaimed my mom. "As in, all the way across the country? That Maine?"

"That's correct."

My mom slammed her hand down on the desk. "This is outrageous. Both Arnold and Azalea have proven that assimilation is possible, and now we're throwing that all away."

Now it was Commander Jensen's turn to lose patience: "Actually, that's not true," he said. "Arnold has done remarkably well. But Azalea has been a different story. We've been monitoring her progress, and there have been certain difficulties. Socially she has not adjusted particularly well. She shows signs of isolation and confusion. And she perpetrated a Zombie Zing on a complete stranger without provocation. What if that person had suffered a heart attack from the trauma? And then sued the U.S. government? Think of the media attention and the public outcry! That is a risk that we are just not willing to take."

My mom was silent. There was nothing she could really say to that, because she knew the commander was right. So I spoke up.

"Will Azalea have to go with the other afterlifes to Maine?" I asked. "Or will she be allowed to stay with the Brantleys?"

"I don't know," said the commander. "She's not like you, Arnold. She hasn't been adopted by them. It's still just a trial period. And frankly, for reasons I've already stated, we're not convinced it can work out in the long run. If she wants, she can continue to live with them for the time being, and we can see how things proceed from here. But ultimately, it's Dr. Grasmere's call."

My mom stood up. "We've taken up enough of your time. Thank you very much for seeing us; we greatly appreciate it."

"Of course," said Commander Jensen. He shook hands with my dad as we all walked to the door. "As I'm sure you know, I wish I had better news. Sometimes our most noble experiments don't go as planned. But we'll never reach the heavens if we don't shoot for the stars."

"I think I read that on a T-shirt somewhere," mumbled my dad as we walked to the car.

FOOd FⁱgHT

The last week of school was weird.

In a way, it was really exciting, because I knew these were going to be the last days I ever got to be at Bernard J. Frumpstein Elementary School. But it was also scary, because I was going to have to go to Shirley R. Flimpton Junior High School next year, and it was big, and there were tons of kids there I didn't know, and in case you forgot, I was a *zombie*. Yeah, there was that.

So of course everyone had a lot to think about, but there were two things on people's minds most of all: The first was Evan, who was clearly a little worn out from his treatment, but seemed to be doing okay; and the second was Azalea, who had officially told everyone that she was probably, almost definitely, going back to the Territory after the school year was over.

Evan had a pass to get out of gym, but otherwise, it was business as usual for him. We all knew he didn't want any extra attention, so we didn't give it to him. But Azalea was a different story. As soon as word got out that she was thinking about leaving, everyone suddenly became super extra nice to her. She was picked first for everything; she was invited to everyone's house after school. Even Mrs. Huggle and the other teachers kept asking her if she needed extra time for homework or tests.

Finally, one day at lunch, Azalea walked into the cafeteria and was looking for a place to sit. I was sitting with Ross, Brett, and Evan—it was a guys-only kind of a day.

"Azalea, come sit with us!" called Kiki from her favorite chair at her favorite table. "I saved you a place!"

"Okay." As Azalea started to head over to Kiki's table, another girl named Cheyenne put her hand out to stop her.

"Hey, Azalea, you never hang at our table," she said. "Won't you sit with us just this once?"

"Um," Azalea said, "okay, I guess."

That was Ross's cue to jump in. "What about us?" he asked. "How about sitting with the fellas?"

Azalea looked confused. "Wait, what?" she said.

Meanwhile, Kiki had gotten up from her seat, walked over to Azalea, and grabbed her by the hand. "I asked first," she said, "and that's all there is to it."

Now Cheyenne got up. "Stop acting like what you say goes all the time, Kiki," she said. "You're not the boss of us, you know. And Azalea sits with you all the time. Let her make up her own mind for once."

Kiki glared at Cheyenne. "She *has* made up her mind, and she wants to sit with us."

"She said she wanted to sit with *us*!" Cheyenne said, her face turning red. By now, everyone had stopped eating and was paying close attention. It wasn't very often that someone stood up to Kiki—in fact, it was never—and no one wanted to miss it.

Ross snickered and elbowed me in the shoulder. "This is one fight I don't want to get in the middle of," he said.

"Me neither," I said.

"And definitely me neither," Evan added.

While Kiki and Cheyenne stared at each other, no one seemed to notice that Azalea was off to the side, stuck there, looking more and more uncomfortable. "Guys?" she said. "Guys? Please don't argue."

Unfortunately, they were too busy arguing to hear her. Kiki thrust her chin out. "Azalea is sitting with me and my friends, and that's final. We really like her and have been her friends ever since she got here, so that's just the way it is."

"FINE," Cheyenne said, almost yelling. She started to retreat to her table, then turned around and marched back up to Azalea. "But you're sitting with us tomorrow, and there's nothing Kiki can do or say about it, and THAT'S final."

"WHATEVER," said Kiki, raising her voice a notch higher than Cheyenne's. "Come on, Azalea, let's go have lunch."

"No, thank you," Azalea said quietly.

And this time, people really paid attention.

Kiki looked stunned. "*No?* What do you mean, no?"

"I mean, no." Azalea put down her tray of jelly beans on someone's table and started to walk out of the cafeteria. Then she changed her mind and turned around.

"I appreciate everyone trying to be so nice to me, I really do," she said. Her voice was still really quiet at first, but it got louder as she went on. "And I understand you all want me to feel at home here. But, uh . . . well . . . to be honest with all of you, the nicer you are, the less at home I feel." She turned to Kiki. "Thank you for wanting to make me feel welcome at your table. But when there's an argument about where I should sit, it actually doesn't make me feel welcome. It makes me feel like some sort of prize that people are fighting over. To be honest, I never wanted you guys to treat me any differently. I just want to be treated like a normal person. Even though I know I can never be a normal person."

"Hey, she sounds like me," Evan whispered, and he was absolutely right.

Azalea just stood there, as if waiting for someone to respond. But no one did. Everyone just sat kind of frozen in place. The only person who reacted in any way was Kiki. She didn't move, but I could see her eyes well up with tears. Finally, without a word, she went and sat back at her table.

Finally, Ross's friend Brett broke the ice. "So what you're saying is, you want us to treat you like we would anyone else?"

Azalea nodded. "Yes, please."

"Okay, I can do that." He stood up. "Yo, Zombieface, why don't you go get a suntan, for crying out loud? You look like a cross between a marshmallow and a stick figure."

Brett laughed at his own bad joke, and his irritating friends followed, including Ross, who added a lame line of his own. "Hey, tomorrow I heard they're serving zombie sweat for lunch! No, thanks, I'll take the fish sticks!" Of course they all cracked up all over again.

Azalea looked shocked—I was pretty sure that wasn't what she'd had in mind. I could feel my own zombie blood start to boil. I stood up. "Hey, guys," I said. "She said she wanted to be treated like a normal person."

Brett laughed harder. "Ha! Have you met us? This *is* how we treat normal people!"

"Well, maybe that's the problem," I said. "Maybe you don't know how to treat anyone well, normal or otherwise."

Kiki stood up, her eyes still a little watery. I was sure she was going to back me up, because she had just been made to feel a little vulnerable herself. But instead, she said, "Arnold, you're overreacting. People make fun of each other all the time. That's what treating people normally means."

I stared at her. "No, it doesn't. What Azalea was saying was that people who are different don't want to be treated differently. And you're right, making fun of people is fine and fun sometimes, but if you make fun of someone *because* they're different, then that's wrong." I paused for a second. "And this time, I'm sorry to tell you, your boyfriend is wrong, too."

I may have put a little extra emphasis on the word *boyfriend*, but I can't quite be sure.

I waited for Kiki to say something, but she didn't. Instead, she just stared at me. So Ross decided to chime in. "Whoa, Arnold," he said. "What are you, like, all of a sudden the expert on human behavior or something? I mean, you're not even human!"

He waited for another laugh, but this time, none came.

"I know I'm not even human," I told him. "I'm an afterlife human, otherwise known as a zombie. And so is Azalea. And maybe it's time for both of us to realize that and go back to where we actually, truly do belong."

"Wait a second," Evan said. "Now let's everyone just

stop saying stuff they don't mean. Arnold, of course you belong here. You're my best friend, and I need you now more than ever, for obvious reasons. And Ross, if you want to be friends with us, you're going to have to stop saying dumb stuff. You, too, Brett. Just...everyone please stop saying dumb stuff!"

Evan slumped back in his seat, exhausted from the effort of saying his piece. But it worked.

"Sorry, everyone," Ross said, shuffling his feet.

"Yeah, me, too," Brett mumbled, staring at the floor.

A small smile crossed Evan's lips. "What about you, Arnold? Are you going to take back what you said, too? About, you know, maybe leaving?"

I hesitated for a second. "I need to think about it."

"Well, don't think about it too long," Evan said.

"I'll try not to."

Okay, I admit it—I was being a little overdramatic right then. But it was how I felt. I wasn't sure right at that moment that I wanted to be there anymore.

And I was also pretty sure that Azalea had made up her mind for good.

good AS NEW

For the next few days after the whole mess at lunch, things got back to semi-normal. People's attention turned to graduation, which was happening that Friday. Evan was busy sending out invitations to his end-of-year party, which was happening the night of the graduation. And everyone decided that it was just best to not talk about what Azalea and I were thinking in terms of staying out in the world, or going back to the Territory to face our fates with the rest of the zombies.

Then, on Wednesday night, the phone rang in our house. After my mom answered it, I heard her say, "Arnold? Phone call for you."

Phone call for *me*? That was a new one. No one ever called me. No one ever called anyone. People just snapped and chatted and texted and 'grammed. Except for me, because I didn't have a phone yet. My parents told me I could get one for the next school year. If I was still there, that is.

I picked up the phone. "This is Arnold Z. Ombee speaking."

I heard Evan cackling on the other end. "Ha! So formal! Hey, Arnold. What's going on?"

"Oh, you know, not much. Reading and eating jelly beans. The usual."

"Cool."

There were a few seconds of silence. It seemed like Evan was just as unfamiliar with talking on a phone as I was.

Finally I said, "Uh, Evan? Did you call for any particular reason?"

I could hear him breathing. (He couldn't hear me breathing, for obvious reasons.) "Oh!" he said, as if that was a surprising question. "Oh, right, I did! Uh, actually, what I wanted to know was if maybe you wanted to come to the hospital with me tomorrow after school?"

"Sorry, what?"

"I wanted to know if you wanted to come to the hospital with me tomorrow. It's my last treatment, and I thought it might be cool to have a few friends there with me to keep me company."

Whoa. I didn't see that coming. "Of course," I told Evan. "I'd love to come."

He laughed. "You'd *love* to come? Nobody ever loves going to a hospital, trust me."

"You know what I mean."

"Have you ever been to a hospital before?"

I thought for a second. "You mean, not including the infirmary where I was created?"

Evan laughed. "Yeah, not including that."

"I guess not. I mean, we don't get sick, remember?"

"What about when you ate chocolate pudding?"

"Oh yeah, good point." Evan was referring to the time right after I'd started in school, when all the kids in class made me eat a bite of chocolate pudding. That didn't go well. "But I only went to the nurse's office that time," I reminded him. "I just had to rest and I was fine."

"Oh. Well, I think maybe it's time you visited a real

live hospital, and you can come as my guest."

"I'd be honored," I said. "Thank you for asking."

And so, the next day after school, Evan's mom picked me up in their big blue minivan. Kiki was already in the car, and so was Sarah Anne.

"Where's Ross?" I asked Kiki.

"Soccer practice," she said.

Is it wrong that I was glad to hear that?

"I don't think Evan wanted him to come, anyway," Kiki added.

"No comment," Evan said.

Is it wrong that I was glad to hear that, too?

Sarah Anne was looking out the window, holding her letter board but not saying anything. I was glad to see her. She was always calm.

"Hi, Sarah Anne," I said. She waved back without taking her eyes away from the window.

It took about fifteen minutes to drive to the hospital. Nobody spoke much, so we listened to the radio. It always amazes me how people don't like silence very much. I think silence is really peaceful, but the world seems to prefer noise. I'm not sure why.

As we were pulling into the hospital parking lot, Evan's mom said, "Okay, guys, this is how it's going to work. Once we check Evan in, he'll go into the treatment room. I don't think you all will be allowed in there, but we'll find out. If not, we can go to the cafeteria and get snacks while we wait. Afterward, we can meet back up in the waiting room while Evan finishes up. Sound like a plan?"

We all nodded, of course. It wasn't as though anyone was going to disagree, that's for sure.

We walked into the hospital, and went through a door marked **PEDIATRIC ONCOLOGY**. I knew what that meant.

Children with cancer.

Sure enough, as soon as we got in there, I saw a bunch of children. Some had hair. Some didn't. Some were skinny, some weren't. Some looked sad, others were laughing. They looked like regular kids, mostly, until I realized that they were in the same fight that Evan was. The fight of their lives.

A young girl came over to us. She was hooked up to some kind of machine, but it was the type that allowed her to still walk around. She hugged Evan, and he hugged her back. She was bald.

"This is Evelyn," he told us. "She's my friend. We thought it was funny that our names sounded alike."

Evelyn smiled shyly. "Hi," she said, shaking hands with each of us.

Sarah Anne pointed at letters on her board. Evelyn looked confused.

"She wants to know how you're feeling," I translated.

"Oh!" Evelyn said. "Tell her I'm feeling pretty good today."

Kiki shook her head. "Oh no, we don't have to. She can hear perfectly fine. She just prefers to communicate by pointing at letters."

"Oh!" Evelyn said again. Then she looked at Sarah Anne. "I'm feeling pretty good. Thanks for asking."

Sarah Anne pointed at her letters again, but this time much slower, so Evelyn could follow along.

YOU ARE BRAVE.

Evelyn gave a short giggle. "Not really. I'm just a person who got sick."

"Stuff happens to everyone," Evan said. He was addressing no one in particular, but I think he might have been talking to me. "And we have two choices: We deal with it, or we don't."

"I agree," Kiki said. "But some people have harder stuff to deal with than other people."

"But we deal with it," Evan repeated.

"Yup," Evelyn said.

Sarah Anne picked up her board and pointed. IT'S CALLED LIFE.

Everyone turned to me, since I hadn't said anything in a while.

"Or semi-life," I said.

Everyone laughed except Evelyn, who didn't get it.

While Evan was getting his treatment, we went down to the cafeteria, like Evan's mom had suggested. There were a lot of medical people there, of course, but also a lot of families and friends, probably doing what we were doing: waiting for someone we cared about to get better.

They didn't sell jelly beans, and I forgot to bring some, so I just sipped water while Kiki and Sarah Anne had ice cream sandwiches.

"Nothing like eating healthy at the hospital," joked Mrs. Brantley. She was making a lot of jokes, trying to stay relaxed, but I could tell how nervous she was. After the snack, we went back to the waiting room. "You guys hang out in here," Mrs. Brantley told us. "I'll be in with Evan. We should be back in about twenty minutes."

Kiki, Sarah Anne, and I did as we were told. There was a TV playing, but none of us watched it. Another man was in there, reading his phone. It was quiet until Kiki turned to me and said, out of the blue, "So are you staying or going?"

It was the first time anyone had directly brought that up since the argument in the cafeteria.

"I honestly don't know," I said.

Kiki nodded. "Okay, I'll take that," she said.

That was it for the talking until Mrs. Brantley came back about fifteen minutes later. "Evan's done," she said. "He's ready to see you guys."

We walked through a set of white double doors and into a room where he was sitting in a reclining chair with his feet up. He looked comfortable, but I could tell from his face that he wasn't.

"Good as new," he said in a hoarse voice.

"Really?"

He gave a weak laugh, then shrugged. "Who knows? They did some tests; we'll find out later. But no more treatments, and that's the main thing." He looked at his mom. "Can we go?"

"Absolutely," said Evan's mom, and she helped her son to his feet. Evan went over to Evelyn, who was lying on another table with something sticking out of her arm. They hugged. She saw us and waved with a smile. We waved back.

"She's got a ways to go," Evan told us as we left. "But she'll be fine, I just know it."

"Time to go home," said Mrs. Brantley.

"You're not kidding," said Evan.

I wasn't exactly sure where my home was, but I knew one thing.

I didn't want to leave my friends.

mR. CITIzENSHIp

The next day was a big one.

At school, it was graduation. Well, technically it was called a "Moving-Up Ceremony," because we were really just a bunch of sixth graders who were going to junior high school next year, but they made a pretty big deal out of it. All the parents came, and they gave everyone a nice certificate, and our principal—who was named Dr. Principal, if you can believe that—gave a very nice speech about how "she's been in education for a long time, but this was one of the most special groups of kids she'd ever had."

We were all pretty sure she said that every year.

At the end, they gave out some awards. A girl named Tanya Francis got the Math Award. A boy named Brian Santore got the Spanish Award. A girl name Rebecca Hanson got the English Award.

And a boy named Arnold Z. Ombee got the Citizenship Award.

That's right. You heard correctly.

Arnold Z. Ombee.

When I heard my name called, it didn't quite sink in at first. Only when my brother Lester smacked me on the back, and his girlfriend Darlene pinched me on the cheek, and my parents hugged me, did I realize, *Hey, wait a second, they just called my name.*

I stood up and people started clapping.

I walked to the front of the auditorium as I heard Dr. Principal's voice: "Arnold has exemplified what it means to be a good citizen here at Bernard J. Frumpstein Elementary School. He was the typical new kid, except he wasn't typical at all. He was, and is, very much his own person. And we are very grateful to him for allowing us to realize that our differences are to be celebrated, not feared."

I stepped up onto the stage and shook Dr. Principal's hand as she handed me a special framed certificate. "Do you want to say anything?" she said into my ear as people clapped. "We generally invite the Citizenship Award winner to say a few words."

"Um . . . I guess so," I said.

She stepped back from the microphone, and I stepped toward it. The crowd hushed.

"Uh, I just wanted to say thank you to Dr. Principal and everyone. When I first started coming to school, I was a little nervous—or a lot nervous, I guess—and you guys made it so much easier." I paused for a second and saw Azalea sitting in the fourth row with Evan and his parents. "Both Azalea and I grew up very differently from the rest of you, as you guys know. And so, thank you again for making us both feel so welcome here. And good luck to everyone at junior high school."

People started clapping again as I went back to my seat. I glanced over at Azalea to try and get a sense of what she was thinking. But Mr. Brantley was leaning forward, and I couldn't see her.

After the ceremony was over, I accepted a ton of congratulations from a ton of people. Evan and his parents were among them, of course. Azalea was kind of lagging behind them a little, like she didn't want to interrupt. Eventually, I went over to where she was standing.

"Hey," I said. "Are you going to be at Evan's party?"

"Of course," she said. "I live there, remember?"

"Oh yeah. Well, I guess I'll see you there."

"Okay."

"Okay."

I paused. "Have you thought any more about—"

"Kind of," she said, interrupting, "but kind of not."

"Okay."

"Okay."

And then everyone hugged the teachers, and said how much we would miss one another, and took pictures, and had more cookies and cupcakes and juice. And Azalea and I mingled, and ate our jelly beans, and kind of did the same things as everyone else, and kind of not.

A Better party
than the Last one

Of course Evan's party had popcorn, since it's his favorite thing in the world. And of course we all jumped on his trampoline, since he was the only one of our friends who actually had a trampoline. And of course, there were healthy snacks, because that's just how Mrs. Brantley is. And also of course, no one ate them.

Halfway through the pizza, the music was blaring and a few kids were jumping around (the sixth-grade version of dancing, even though they weren't technically in sixth grade anymore, as of five hours earlier). A bunch of other kids were taking pictures of one another with the phones they'd gotten as graduation presents. I spotted Evan in the corner, sitting by himself. At first, I thought the only reason he could have been alone was because he wanted to be alone. It was his party, after all! But maybe he didn't actually want to be alone. So I went over and sat down next to him.

"Hey," I said. "You good?"

He half nodded. "Yeah, I'm pretty good. Just a little tired. Also, I have to be a little careful about not being surrounded by people all the time."

"Ah, that makes sense," I said.

We sat there for a few more seconds, and then I added, "Do you remember the first time I came to a party at your house? Your birthday party?"

"Of course I remember! You ended up jumping out the window."

"Yeah," I said. "I sure did." Evan's dad was my enemy back then, and he was trying to catch me. Things had sure changed.

"I just want to say," I told him, "that I really appreciate everything you've done for me since I've gotten here."

"You mean, including when you first got on the bus and I flicked you on the back of your neck?"

"Totes, even including that."

Evan chuckled slightly.

"What are you laughing at?" I asked.

"I'm laughing at the fact that you now say 'totes.' You really are fitting in nicely."

Ross came running over with a basketball. "You guys up for a game?"

Evan and I looked at each other. "Uh," he said, "my doctor doesn't think it's a great idea, to be honest with you."

Ross looked embarrassed. "Oh, shoot, sorry I asked!"

"No, I'm glad you asked," Evan said. "Maybe soon."

Ross turned to me. "What about you, Ombee the Zombie? You in?"

I sighed. "Do I have a choice?"

"Not really!" Ross said, laughing. "Let's do this!"

And so off I went, to flounder around on the basketball court with real humans who could actually run and jump. Every time I got the ball, my only job was to get rid of it as quickly as I could. And on defense, my only job was to not trip over my own two feet.

But somehow, with Brett, Kiki, and a very tall boy named Kristof all on my team, we managed to win, 21–17. After the game we all high-fived one another, which would have hurt a lot, if zombies could feel pain.

"Good playing, Ombee," said Kristof. "Way to hang in there."

He said it to me just the way he said it to all the other kids on the team. Which must have meant he just saw me as another person. No better, no worse, no weirder, no smarter, no zombie-er. Just another person.

Which is all I ever really wanted.

"You, too, Kristof," I said, but he'd already moved on to the next teammate.

Which was fine with me.

"TIME FOR CAKE!" called Evan's mom.

"WOO-HOO!" answered everybody.

The huge cake was chocolate with butterscotch icing—Evan's favorite.

But before we could eat any of that probably delicious food, Mrs. Brantley banged a fork against a glass about ten times. "Could I get everyone's attention? Everyone, please? Everyone means EVERYONE." After the fourth "everyone," people finally piped down. "This is a very exciting day for all of us," Evan's mom continued, "and you should all be so proud of your accomplishment as Frumpstein Elementary graduates. But for one young graduate, this day is even more exciting. And I'd like to invite that graduate to tell you all why. My son, Evan Brantley."

Everyone turned to Evan, who looked at his mom as if to say, *Are you seriously making me do this right now?* But she just smiled down at him, and his dad said, "Come on, Ev. Everyone will want to know."

So Evan shrugged, sighed, and rose up off his picnic bench. Then he stood in front of everyone and said only seven words.

"The doctor thinks I should be fine."

It's possible that the reason he said only seven words was because by the time he got to the seventh word, people were already hooting and hollering and yelling stuff like "YAAAY!" and "EVAN ROCKS!!!!"

It took about five minutes for Mr. Brantley to calm everyone down.

"I want you all to know something," he said, with tears in his eyes. "As wonderful as this news is, it does not mean the fight is over. With something like this, the fight is never over. But if there is one person I know who is up for a fight, it's my son Evan. And with all of you to give him incredible help, and support, and friendship along the way, I know it's a fight he will win."

There was cheering all over again, and Evan was swarmed all over again, too. But he managed to catch my eye.

"Friendship along the way," he said. "That means you."

I nodded. "You bet it does."

Then cake was served.

I had jelly beans.

They were delicious.

HOME, PART I

I was so happy when Evan said he didn't have cancer anymore.

I cheered like everyone else. I toasted him like everyone else. And then I ate jelly beans like Arnold, while everyone else ate cake.

It was a really nice party.

Then, the next morning, at breakfast, I told Evan and his parents that I had something to say.

"I've made up my mind. I'd like to go back to the Territory."

Mr. and Mrs. Brantley looked at each other. "Are you sure?" asked Mrs. Brantley.

"I'm sure."

Evan took a bite of his tofu pancakes (no more pizza and cake for him). "I just want to say, um, that I think it was really brave that you agreed to come here."

"I don't think so," I told him. "I wasn't brave enough

to figure out a way to belong here and be comfortable."

"Different people belong different places," Evan said.

"My place is back home with my friends," I said.

The next morning, there was a knock on the door. I opened it, and Dr. Grasmere was standing there.

"Ready to go?" he asked.

I nodded.

"I see we have company," he said, pointing. I looked behind him.

Arnold and his family were standing in the driveway, outside his car.

"We want to come with you," Arnold said.

We drove back to the Territory. I could tell things were different as soon as we drove through the gates. Most of the buildings had boards over the windows. Half the pods were gone.

"What's going on?" I asked Dr. Grasmere.

"The removal has begun," he said.

"Are Berstus and Frumpus still here?"

"They're leaving today."

As we drove through the gates, Arnold reached over and held my hand.

"Can you stop the car?" I asked, spotting my old pod.

Dr. Grasmere turned around from his spot in the front passenger seat. "Not right now. We have a lot to do."

"I would really like it if you stopped the car."

He hesitated for a second, then nodded to the driver. We stopped.

I jumped out of the car, with Arnold right behind me. We ran into the pod. Berstus and Frumpus were both there, sitting on their benches, reading. They looked up at the same time and saw me. Both their mouths dropped open.

"Azalea," Berstus said. "My goodness, you came back."

"And Arnold, you came back, too," Frumpus said.

"I'm staying," I said.

"I'm not," Arnold said.

We all hugged.

"I'm so sorry," Arnold said. "But I have a new home."

"We understand," Frumpus said.

"I hope you're not too scared," Arnold said.

Berstus shook her head. "We're not scared at all."

Arnold looked surprised. "You're not?"

"No," Frumpus said. "This will be something new. We have been told that we are moving to a nice place where we will continue to learn ways in which we can help society."

"I can vouch for that," said Dr. Grasmere, who I didn't even realize was standing there. "They are going to all be very well taken care of. This is the beginning of an exciting new chapter in the history of this program."

Arnold stared at Dr. Grasmere. "Why should we suddenly start trusting you now?" he asked. "You haven't exactly been our best friend up till now."

Dr. Grasmere sighed. "I understand," he said. "You must remember, I always had the nation's best interests in mind. Sometimes that led me into decisions I regret. But seeing Azalea perform in the school play was truly eye-opening for me, and moving." He smiled. "This program has always been near and dear to my heart, and I realize now that the best course of action is to treat everyone with respect. Humans and not-quite-humans alike."

Arnold looked unsure. "I really want to believe you."

"You can," said Dr. Grasmere. Then he looked at me and smiled. It was the first time his smile didn't scare me. "I hope you do as well, Azalea."

I had already made up my mind. I felt I had no choice.

"I'm ready," I said.

I hugged Mr. and Mrs. Brantley good-bye.

Then I hugged Evan and thanked him for everything.

"You are an incredible person," I told him.

"You are an incredible zombie," he told me. He had tears in his eyes.

Zombies don't cry, but humans do.

I turned to Arnold.

"Please stay in touch with us," I said.

"I will," he told me. "And I'll try to make you all proud."

"You already have," I told him.

HOME, PART II

So that's the story of how one zombie ended up with a human family, while another zombie went back to her zombie family.

Somewhere out there, there's a family for everyone, right?

So I guess that's it, then. Thanks for reading.

Oh, wait! I have one more interesting thing to tell you.

One of the first things we did that summer was go to an amusement park.

Have you ever been to an amusement park?

They're very amusing.

You play games, and take rides, and run around, and human people eat all sorts of colorful stuff, like this thing called cotton candy, which is half cotton and half candy and is just more proof that humans are stranger than zombies.

Anyway, if you ask me, amusement parks kind of sum up American society in general: noisy, fun, tiring, and full of freedom to do whatever you want, even if it's not the smartest decision in the world (like going on rides until you throw up).

I went with Evan, Kiki, and Sarah Anne. Lester and Darlene were there, too, but they went off by themselves. Ross didn't come—not because I didn't want him to, but because he and Kiki weren't boyfriend and girlfriend anymore.

I know, right?

When I asked Kiki what happened, she said, "Ross is an intriguing person, but I would much rather keep my options open than be tied down, especially as we head into junior high."

When I asked Ross what happened, he said, "Yeah, whatever, I just was like, yeah, you know, whatever."

I think those two answers pretty much sum up why that couple was never going to work.

Kiki seemed delighted with her newfound freedom. In fact, she might have been having the most fun at the park out of everyone. And she could ride a roller coaster ten times without feeling sick, which everyone thought was pretty impressive. Evan rode it once and was paler than me.

At the end of a long, hot, and wonderful day, my parents came to pick us all up.

"How was it?" they asked.

"Amazing," we all mumbled. We were too tired to say anything else.

But here's why I wanted to tell you this story.

As we got into the car and drove home from the amusement park, I leaned against the window. My parents were chatting, there was music playing pretty quietly, and I closed my eyes and thought about the day. And then I thought about the day that the Kinders found me, and everything that had happened to me since then. And I realized that I could remember everything! My memories were all there! And memories are important. They're how we keep track of our lives, after all.

And that got me thinking how lucky I was that I even got to *be* alive. I think everyone's lucky to be alive, don't you? Even if it's only a certain kind of alive, like me.

So, yeah, I thought about all that stuff. And it was a lot to think about, which might explain what happened next, which was incredible.

It was actually kind of magical, even.

It was one of the things that I had always been told was impossible, like eating cake, or having a heartbeat or complete memories. And the fact that it happened made me think that maybe, just maybe, one day I could be a real person after all.

Can you guess what it was?

Okay, I'll tell you.

I fell asleep.

ACKNOWLEdgmENTS

Arnold and all his friends would like to thank:

Brianne Johnson and Allie Levick, for making this series happen.

Anna Bloom, for making this series so much better.

Everyone at Scholastic, Scholastic Book Clubs, and Scholastic Book Fairs, for taking this series out into the world.

Parents, teachers, librarians, media specialists, volunteers, grandparents, aunts, uncles, and book lovers, for getting this series into the hands of young readers.

And mostly, to those young readers themselves, who still—amazingly and thrillingly enough—READ.

A HUGE ZOMBIE HUG TO EVERY ONE OF YOU!

ABOUT THE AUTHOR

© Suzanne Sheridan

TOMMY GREENWALD is the author of many books for children, including the CrimeBiters! series, the Charlie Joe Jackson series, and the football novel *Game Changer*. This is his first series for zombies.

SINK YOUR TEETH INTO CRIMEBITERS!

I KNOW WHAT YOU'RE THINKING.

You're thinking that just because I love crime fighters, vampires, and dogs, I made up the whole thing about having a crime-fighting vampire dog.

Well, I didn't. It's all true. This story is so wild that I don't think ANYBODY could have made it up. Not even Elroy Evans, writer of the greatest vampire books ever.

Turn the page for a special sneak peek!

INTRODUCTION

PROFILE*

Name: Jimmy Bishop (me)

Age: 11

Occupation: Kid

Interests: Crime fighters, vampires, dogs, not girls

*STOP! POLICE!—which is my all-time-favorite TV show, by the way—does these cool profiles of all the new characters on every episode. So I thought I'd do it too. It's not like I'm stealing the idea or anything. Just paying tribute to it. There's a difference. I think.

4:56 P.M.

DAD PULLED INTO THE DRIVEWAY, HONKING HIS horn.

"Get in! We're late."

We're late?!? WE?!?!

"Where were you?" I asked, but I could tell he was totally distracted. "Dad! Stop staring at your phone!"

"I'm waiting for an important call," he said, which I guess was his version of an apology.

FACT: Dads are horrible at apologizing.

On the way to the shelter neither of us talked for a few minutes.

"So can I get any dog I want?" I asked.

"Sure," said my dad. "As long as it's between fourteen and nineteen months old, and weighs between twenty-five and thirty-five pounds."

"That's not exactly *any* dog, Dad," I grumbled, as the GPS lady told us to take a left.

"Mom talked to somebody at work who's a big-time animal lover," Dad said. "She says we should get a dog who's past the crazy puppy phase but still young enough to be fun and playful. And size-wise, I don't want one of those tiny, fluffy dogs that movie stars put in their pocketbooks, but I also don't want one of those monster dogs that take up the entire couch."

Those ground rules sounded a little strict to me. What if I wanted to get a dog that was thirty-seven pounds?

"But Dad—"

"No buts."

He turned the radio on and started drumming on the steering wheel. Conversation officially over.

5:06 P.M.

WHEN I WALKED INTO THE NORTHPORT ANIMAL Rescue Foundation (otherwise known as Northport ARF!), dogs and cats of all shapes and sizes tried to get my attention. It was like a kickball game and I was the captain, and they were all yelling, "PICK ME! PICK ME!" But it wasn't a kickball game. It was real life, and they all wanted me to take them home so they could feel safe and warm and loved.

"Look!" I yelled. "They're so cute! I want all of them!"

Even my dad seemed to be affected by all the cuteness. He actually smiled a few times. But he shook his head. "Nice try, Jimmy. You know the deal. One dog." He pointed at a beagle that was jumping in circles. "And nothing too crazy. We don't want our house ripped to shreds."

FACT: If you consider yourself not that popular of a person, go to an animal shelter. You will feel really popular really fast.

I noticed a cocker spaniel that was wagging its tail and barking. "How about that one?"

My dad shook his head again. "I'm not sure I can listen to that barking all night. And the neighbors would hate us."

I soon discovered that my dad had a reason to turn down pretty much every dog I pointed at or played with.

"Too big."

"Too small."

"Too hairy." "Too smelly." "Too loud." "Too sleepy." "Too young." "Too playful."

My dad was "too annoying."

I knew it. This whole thing was a setup.

I was about to give up when we rounded the last corner of the last room in the whole place and saw this dark, tiny cage in the corner. All I could see were two bright lights shining straight at me. As I walked closer, I realized they weren't lights at all. They were eyes.

I ran over to the cage and looked in. There was a scruffy little dog just lying there. He looked like a combination of a thousand different breeds—he had spots, he had stripes, his eyes were two different colors, his ears were two different shapes, and he had a big black streak of fur right down his back, almost like a cape. He was wagging his tail sleepily, and he had the cutest, saddest face I'd ever seen.

In other words, he was *awesome*.

I ran over to one of the guys who worked there. "Hi! Is this dog available? Is he nice?"

The guy nodded. "Oh, she's a bit of a loner. Likes to sleep all day, but she's wide awake at night. The doc thinks her eyes are supersensitive to light for some reason. A total sweetheart, though."

Oh! So he was a she. Hmmm. I'd always imagined having a boy dog. Oh well.

"How old is she?"

"About a year and a half."

"How much does she weigh?"

The guy scratched his head. "What is this, the third degree? I'd say about thirty pounds."

Yes! Perfect.

"Dad! I found her! I found her!"

"Oh yeah?"

"Come quick!"

He sighed and walked over to the cage to take a look. After about a minute, he asked the worker guy, "Can you please take her out so we can say hi?"

The guy opened the cage and brought the dog over. As I started petting her, she looked right into my eyes. I could swear she was smiling! She seemed sleepy, but she was sooooooo cute! She didn't look like any dog I'd ever seen before.

"What kind of dog is she?" I asked.

"A whole lot of everything," said the guy.

"What's her name?"

The guy laughed. "Whatever you want it to be."

"Let me take a look," my dad said. The guy handed him the-dog-with-no-name. My dad stood there for a few seconds, just kind of staring at her. He didn't look very enthusiastic. In fact, he looked like he was reconsidering the whole thing. I started to think this whole dog thing would never happen.

All of a sudden, the dog stretched, pulled her head back, and sneezed right in my dad's face.

That's right. You heard me.

FACT: If you're in the middle of adopting a dog, try to make sure it doesn't sneeze in your dad's face.

"BLECH!" my dad said. He scowled as he handed the dog to me, while the worker guy tried not to laugh.

"Dad?" I said, but I knew it was over. There was no way we were getting this dog.

Then my dad's phone rang.

He looked at the phone. Then he looked at me.

"You better get it," I said.

As my dad walked off down the hall, I waited there with the dog still in my hands. She was pretty heavy, so I sat down on the floor. "Why did you have to sneeze right then?" I asked her, but she wouldn't answer.

Follow all the cases of the CrimeBiters, and the dog that may or may not be a crime-fighting vampire.

UNDEAD AND ON THE RUN!

A zombie kid faces the ultimate test: making it through human elementary school.

scholastic.com

GREENWALD